PICK 'N MIX

A collection of short stories

by

HELEN SPRING

Gotham Books

30 N Gould St.
Ste. 20820, Sheridan, WY 82801
https://gothambooksinc.com/

Phone: 1 (307) 464-7800

© 2025 *Helen Spring*. All rights reserved.

No part of this book may be reproduced, stored in a retrieval system, or transmitted by any means without the written permission of the author.

Published by Gotham Books (April 10, 2025)

ISBN: 979-8-3492-7630-9 (H)
ISBN: 979-8-3493-6546-1 (P)
ISBN: 979-8-3493-6547-8 (E)

Because of the dynamic nature of the Internet, any web addresses or links contained in this book may have changed since publication and may no longer be valid.

The views expressed in this work are solely those of the author and do not necessarily reflect the views of the publisher, and the publisher hereby disclaims any responsibility for them.

Table of Contents

THE ROWAN TREE 1

THE PATIO GHOST 26

NEW WINDOWS 30

THE BRIDE CLOTH 35

TURNING POINT 39

BEST SERVED COLD 46

SUMMER DESTINY 54

RESOLUTION 57

WITHOUT A FLAW 65

MICHAEL 70

MOTHER LOVE 77

CHRISTO'S LESSON 82

WHITE BEAR LAKE 89

THE ANGEL 95

THE ROWAN TREE

———◆———

1985

The Spring Bank Holiday Saturday dawned clear and sunny, upon an unbelieving British public, long conditioned to rainy windswept Whit weekends. Cherry blossom drifted like pink snow in the suburban streets, and lambs gambolled in the fields and fells. The organisers of village fetes, mop fairs and car boot sales stopped worrying about enough people turning up and started to worry instead about the stock lasting out. There was an air of euphoria in the busy streets of market towns and villages, a rush to buy cotton dresses and tee shirts, bedding plants and fishing nets. Families played good humored games as they sat out the motorway traffic jams, strains of Beethoven mingling with rock and pop from a hundred open windows.

Even Charles was affected. 'Beautiful day Sam!' he remarked to the blue Persian cat rubbing against his legs in the kitchen. Sam emitted a plaintive sound.

'All right, all right!' Charles muttered as he scooped out cat food with an air of distaste. He set the dish down in a corner, opened the back door, and stepped out onto the terrace. Charles was an angular, bony man, with a greyish, deprived look. His austere features and aquiline nose gave him a somewhat patrician air, and this effect was heightened by the long, sensitive fingers and his habit of jerking his head slightly to one side before he spoke. A solitary man, he valued his isolation, living with it as one does, with what one cannot change.

Now from the small terrace he appraised the garden. This year it looked as he had intended. After three years of planning, it was repaying his efforts. The young man who came twice a week had carried out his instructions, and all was order and symmetry. Charles felt himself soothed by the sight of the low clipped box hedges which bordered the flower beds. The beds themselves, filled with well-behaved plants spaced at uniform distances and heights like soldiers on parade, gratified his sense of discipline. The serried rows of tulips stood smartly to attention, glowing in the sun. Like a Mozart string quartet or a Jane Austen novel, all was in proportion, all was harmony.

The only problem was the tree. Charles surveyed the offending rowan, which was not in his garden at all, but in the cottage garden which bordered his at the far end. Diseased, the man from the Ministry of Agriculture had said. Must be bad for them to be called in. Not a danger yet, and could be saved, but expensive. Five hundred pounds at least, and could be more. Nice of them to inform him though. Perhaps it was obligatory for a notifiable disease. Charles screwed up his eyes to try and judge the effect on his view if the tree should be removed. He didn't like what he saw. Not only would his graceful background of trees be interrupted, but it would be replaced by a view of the cottage roofs, and probably a glimpse of the semi-detached houses opposite.

He frowned. It could not happen. He would see it did not. According to the man from the Ministry an old man named Gibson owned the cottage. Apparently this Mr. Gibson did not want the tree taken down, but did not want to pay for its treatment and preservation. Perhaps if he offered Mr. Gibson a little financial help? Charles was not rich, his career as a cello soloist was a little chequered, particularly at the moment. But neither was he extravagant, and could easily afford five hundred pounds, especially if it ensured his privacy, and his continued enjoyment of this quite superb view. He would certainly go to see the old man and offer his assistance.

Even though he had decided on his course of action, Charles spent another hour reviewing it. He was not a man inclined to impulse, and an impulse it certainly had been. It was not his tree, and not his responsibility, he argued with himself. He then counter argued that it was surely in his interest to preserve the tree, and that if he did not arrange to do so fairly quickly, he would be away on his next tour of engagements and the tree might well have disappeared by the time he returned. That would be unthinkable, he reasoned, but still, he did not act.

Instead, he returned to the kitchen and made some coffee, and sat in his small lounge drinking it, and rereading the reviews of last Thursday's concert. That critic at the Guardian, - what did it take to please him? Criticism was one thing, but surely 'soulless' was a little over the top? He reached for the Daily Telegraph. It was not much better. Amazingly, at least for once they seemed to be saying the same thing. 'Technical brilliance but lacking in original interpretation'. 'An austere and disciplined performance rather than a lyrical one.' He sighed, he had read it all before, a hundred times during his career. What was wrong with technical excellence anyway? It was true, he was austere and disciplined in his approach, that was how he read the music, how he experienced it. He wondered if his mother had seen the reviews, and knew she would have made sure she did. He would have a letter next week suggesting she come to stay again, or that he should visit her. He considered possible excuses. Pressure of rehearsals and engagements was wearing a bit thin, especially since she followed his career so closely. He had not seen much of her since he split up with Anna. His mother and Anna had always been close. He closed his eyes and let his mind dwell on Anna. It was a pleasant prospect. No-one could believe it when he had broken off the engagement, he had hardly believed it himself. Ah well! Water under the bridge. He picked up the paper and read the reviews again. Perhaps he should stick to Bach and Mozart, later composers invariably led to searing comment on his interpretation. The problem was that the public always wanted the

Elgar, even though after Du Pre it was impossible for anyone else, apart perhaps from Rostropovich......

Eventually the combination of the warm sunny day and his decision to play benefactor prodded Charles outdoors again. Although his decision to help in the matter of the tree was founded on self-interest, he neither admitted nor even realised this. He therefore set off in a benignly philanthropic mood, to find old Mr. Gibson's cottage.

***

As cottages go, it was something of a non-starter. It had no thatch, no beams, no white plastered walls, or roses round the door. What it did have was an air of genteel malaise, a tiny brick house, with small window panes and a peeling green front door.

In answer to Charles' knock, there was a rasping of bolts, and after what seemed a long time, the door opened two inches. Charles peered forward. 'Mr. Gibson?' he enquired.

'Who wants 'im?'

'My name is Charles Erskine. I live in the house at the bottom of your garden. Mr. Chalmers from the Ministry came to see me about your rowan tree. I wondered if I could help?'

The door opened another inch. Charles became aware he was being subjected to scrutiny. He smiled. 'Do you think I could have a word? Could I come in for a moment?'

After some hesitation the door opened. 'If you must.' The old man who had spoken left the doorway and ambled off down the narrow hall, leaving Charles to follow. As they entered the small kitchen, Charles saw that his unwilling host was a big, shambling man, old, and a little bent, but still with an air of strength and vigour. He was dressed in corduroy trousers and a checked shirt with no collar. He had not shaved and had at least two days grizzled stubble on his chin. The face which turned to look at Charles was weather beaten, with heavy creases at the corners of his eyes from glinting against the sun. Yes. A gardener indeed.

Now the eyes took on a baleful look as the old man barked: 'Well, what's it about then?'

'As I explained I live in the house at the bottom of your garden, you may have seen me from time to time, or at least you will have seen Sam, my cat.'

'The big 'ouse? That blue Persian yours is it?'

Charles smiled and admitted that it was.

'I don't care much for cats. '

Charles protested that cats were wonderful pets, and that he and Sam got on very well together.

The old man snorted. 'If that cat were big enough' he said skeptically, 'He'd eat you!'

Charles decided to change the subject. 'About the rowan tree,' he began, and went on to explain the position. The old man heard him out with obvious and increasing animosity. Hastily Charles reiterated that he was here to help, that the loss of the tree would spoil his view, and this meant he had an interest in the matter. He smiled and offered to pay for the treatment and preservation of the tree. To his surprise and dismay the old man was not only ungrateful, he was positively rude.

'That Chalmers 'ad no right, no right at all!' he grumbled. 'Tisn't your tree. Nothin' to do with you.'

Charles bridled. 'He was only doing his job,' he remonstrated, 'After all, it does affect me as well.' The old man stared at him.

'It affects the view from my terrace' Charles explained again. 'That rowan must be over forty feet high, and it makes a big difference.'

The old man glowered. 'Tis my tree,' he said shortly. 'I 'avent decided yet what to do about it. When I 'ave I'll let you know. I don't need no 'elp and nobody's money thank you very much.'

Charles left fuming. So this was what one got for trying to be a good neighbour! God help conservation! His usual philosophy of keeping himself to himself was obviously the right one. He sighed, and wondered again how he would be able to keep his mother at a distance for the next few weeks.

***

Two hours later Tom Gibson pulled the last piece of groundsel from the cabbages and straightened slowly. He felt belligerent since his run-in with Charles Erskine, and his back ached. Odd how the tiredness came so quickly now. He'd seen the day when he could weed ten rows without straightening up, long rows at that, and never a twinge. Getting old, no two ways about it. Still, nice crop of cabbages this year, and Meg would be glad of them for the family. He liked to be able to do something for his daughter, after all she did plenty for him. God knows what would have become of him if Meg hadn't been there after Beth died. Mind you, she was a pest sometimes, always changing the sheets and moving things from where he'd left them. He smiled, just like her Mum. But after Meg's visits the cottage always looked bright and cheerful, just as it did when Beth was alive. Although he grumbled, Tom was grateful. At some deep level of consciousness he was vaguely aware that if it hadn't been for Meg he wouldn't have been able to stay on at the cottage. Couldn't have coped really. He could have made his home with Meg and her family, she'd asked him often enough, but to be honest much as he loved his grandchildren he liked them most in small doses. Anyway, he had to stay here. Fifty four years it had been, since he and Beth moved in after their wedding, and here he would stay till the Lord took him. Here with Beth.

Daft talk! he told himself, Beth wasn't here now. Odd though, how he still felt she was. He was out in the garden and she was in the kitchen, like always. The deep ache rose again in him, a great leaden lump in his chest. Two years now and it was still as bad. Oh Beth, Beth...

Abruptly he turned and made his way back toward the cottage. The small vegetable plot gave way to the enchanting tangle of the flower garden, and he lingered a moment, catching the heavy scent of the gilly flowers, and watching the honey bees at work among the early foxgloves. A riot of pink clematis had woven its way through the vivid blue ceanothus, and the tall tulips fought for survival among the carpet of forget-me-nots and rambling aubrietia.

A sweet rush of memories engulfed him. Beth gathering herbs for the kitchen. Meg at two years old, teetering down the brick path clutching forget-me-nots for Mummy. Beth's delighted smile as she discovered yet more self seeded 'granny's bonnets.' And of course, the rowan tree. He turned to look at it, and there she was, Beth in her favourite spot, sitting beneath the rowan, shelling peas. She laughed a little as she turned towards him, picking up the pods with deft movements, and balancing the colander in her lap. 'This old tree will be here Tom, long after you and I are gone.'

Tom shook his head to erase the image and turned away. The tree was old and diseased, and there was no tree worth five hundred pounds to put right. No matter how much Beth loved it, and whatever that silly bugger Charles Erskine might say. He made his way slowly back to the cottage and into the tiny kitchen. His movements were slow and ungainly as he put on the kettle, and dropped a teabag into the large blue and white striped mug. As he waited, he scrutinized the tree again from the kitchen window. A lovely tree no doubt, but Tom was not romantic about nature. He had spent his whole life growing things, forty four years as a gardener for John Driscoll, at what passed for the nearest thing to a mansion in the village. Forty four years, with only a break during the war. Forty four years battle with weeds and weather, slugs and aphids. Always hard work and always poorly paid. He'd recognised the fireblight as soon as he saw the crinkled brown buds and the slime on the bark of the rowan. Knew it was serious, and had to be notified to the Ministry. It was a pity, but during his time Tom had cut down many trees, grubbed up and thrown away countless plants. He could not feel particularly deeply about the loss of one tree. Not like that silly bugger Charles Erskine.

A shudder of impatience ran through Tom as he poured the boiling water into the mug. Charles Erskine! There's a toffee-nosed name if you like! Some sort of musician, so they say. Cello player, supposed to be quite famous. Well I've never heard of 'im. The idea of earning a living from such an unlikely occupation was entirely beyond Tom's comprehension, and Charles was therefore unacceptable on any terms. Cheeky bugger! Turning up 'ere uninvited, and going on about the tree as if 'e owned it! 'Spoil his view' he said! What do I care if it spoils 'is view? Must have precious little to do if all 'e 'as to worry about is 'is view! Stuck up sod! Talked all the time as if 'e was reading the news, and offering to pay for the tree surgeon. Why should 'e pay? - nothing to do with 'im. Not 'is tree. It's mine, - mine and Beth's. Always 'as been and always will be. The deep ache welled up again, and with it the bitter choking guilt, the guilt that was always there beneath the surface. He should have told her. There were plenty of times when he could have told her, but he hadn't. Now it was too late. He could never explain now.

***

It was several days before the two combatants in the matter of the tree met again. By this time both had had a little more time to reflect. As far as Tom was concerned, these reflections came and went in his mind accompanied by comments like 'silly bugger,' and later 'well at least he wanted to 'elp - took an interest, like'. He also became consumed by a growing curiosity to know more of someone who earned his living by playing a cello. Meanwhile, the tree surgeon was pressing for a decision. If the rowan was to be saved, the treatment had to be done quickly. Tom listened, and agreed time was of the essence, and shut the door on Mr. Chalmers promising an early decision. 'A couple of days that's all'. Of course he didn't need a couple of days. In his heart he had known all along what the decision would be. But coming to terms with it, facing the fact that he had money to spend in such a wasteful and ridiculous way... that would surely take a couple of days. In the event, pure nosey-parker curiosity got the better of him, and only a day later he decided to speak to the silly bugger at the big house. He was keen to see what a cello player's house looked like, a famous one at that. He sat down at the scrubbed table in the kitchen, and wrote Charles Erskine a laborious and ill spelled note.

***

Charles' reflections on the matter of the tree had been much less patient and stoic. For the first time in years he found himself not only angry, but thoroughly disconcerted. The total rejection of his offer of help had come not only as a surprise, but had underlined to him the extent of his insularity. After all it was one thing to choose to live a life of quiet, well ordered solitude, and quite another to be given the cold shoulder, especially by an ignorant, obnoxious old man! Charles was surprised at the strength of his own reactions. 'What on earth does it matter?' he had grumbled to himself on the night of the confrontation, when sleep had deserted him and the conversation with Tom resounded in his head. 'You can live without that tree, if the old duffer decides to have it taken down. Plant something else, fast growing, to repair the view, and let the old man go to hell!' Still, he was annoyed, and the source of that annoyance had little to do with the tree. There had been something about the old man's attitude, faintly dismissive, as if Charles was a slight interruption to all that was important to him. It had been rather like brushing off a fly. The old man had a contained presence about him, an essence of individuality and scope. Charles had seen and felt this only once before in his lifetime, in the company of a great musical talent, a conductor of world- wide renown. How was it that an ignorant old gardener could have the same effect on him? In an odd way he made Charles feel inferior. He brushed away the thought as soon as it crossed his mind. What nonsense! A silly old man! And that awful cottage! Full of dark corners and horse brasses and Toby jugs with 'A present from Torquay' on them! But Charles still felt uncomfortable. Although the cottage was stuffed with shabby worn furniture and cheap knick-knacks, it had had a similar effect on him as the old man. It was like him, all of a piece, together, like a conspiracy. The shabbiness had a unity, the jumble of pottery ornaments and the winking horse brasses had found a harmony, a concordance. It was as if the cottage and its sole inhabitant understood each other, and after many shared experiences had arrived at a mutual respect.

These reflections, so meaningful and poignant in the middle of the night, seemed absurd to Charles in the cold light of day. When he received Tom's note a couple of days later, he therefore had no hesitation in inviting the old man to tea. He put his confused feelings about Tom down to the fact that he had been taken by surprise by his rudeness. On home ground the situation would be different. On the day of Toms visit he therefore felt quite at ease as he put the last touches to the tea tray, making sure everything was in order. The porcelain cups and saucers were precisely laid out, with the teaspoons at a correct angle. The small fancy cakes brought in especially by Mrs. Bates, his capable daily help, were arranged attractively on the cake-stand. Tom Gibson had not made him welcome at his cottage, but that was no reason for behaving in a like manner himself. The old man would see how civilised people behaved, and perhaps learn something. These pompous deliberations gave Charles a quiet satisfaction, reinforced by the subconscious knowledge that his dignified reception and meticulous tea tray would make Tom Gibson thoroughly uncomfortable. Satisfied with his preparations, he decided there was time for a half hour practice period before Tom arrived. Leaving his front door on the latch, he moved to the small study which he used as a music room. He tuned the cello to his satisfaction, and after a short pause, began to play. He began with Albeniz 'Puerta de tierra.' The sweet vibrant sound echoed through the house, but found little response in the arid rooms. The expensive modern furniture, which owed much to black leather, stainless steel and glass, seemed unrelated to the sonorous voice of the cello, and its poignant beauty.

At length Charles leaned back and looked up. To his surprise Tom Gibson stood in the doorway, with a look of amazement on his face and a large bunch of flowers in his hand. The old man's mouth was open. He seemed to find speech difficult. 'Oh! - well then. I hope you did'n mind me comin' in -.' He gestured. 'Door was open see? I just heered the music, I thought you would'n mind.'

'Not at all, do come in, I'm so sorry I didn't hear you, I'm afraid I forgot the time.' Charles tone was conciliatory as he put away the cello and rose to greet the old man. Tom thrust the flowers at him. 'Peace offerin'! For your lady!' he said with a slight grin. 'I was a bit short t'other day.'

Charles was slightly embarrassed. 'How kind! But I'm afraid I don't have a lady,' he murmured, wondering what one did with such a tangle of blowsy blooms. He needn't have worried, as Tom took on the role of arranger. 'Just find me a vase,' he volunteered, 'and I'll put 'em in water, while you brews up!' Thus it came about that old Tom Gibson busied himself in the pristine ultra modern kitchen, looking around all the time with astonishment at the technological miracles it contained, and the gleaming, clutter free surfaces. 'Well I never!' he exclaimed more than once. Charles, making tea and watching with some apprehension for the safety of his crystal bowl in Tom's shaking hands, nevertheless felt a tinge of appreciation. The old man was obviously trying to make amends. They went through to the lounge. Charles put down the tea tray and took the flowers. Undecided for a while, he eventually set them down on a small low table. Extraordinary! Charles had the strangest feeling that the flowers had brought into the room some rare essence, some kind of benevolent power, the same kind of effect he had noticed at the cottage. Or perhaps it was Tom himself? He glanced across at him.

'They're lovely! Did you grow them?'

'Oh yes. From my garden.' The old man eyed the tea tray. 'Well I never!' he said again. Then to Charles' surprise, 'I never did 'ear anythin' so beautiful! When you was playin' like. Never 'eered anythin' like it in my life!'

In spite of himself Charles was flattered. Someone liked his interpretation. Pity Tom wasn't the Guardian critic! He toyed a little with this intriguing thought, before replying: 'Well of course it's my job you know.'

'More'n a job, I'd say!' Tom was vehement. 'Yes indeed! More'n a job! A gift, I'd say. Yes, a gift! A real artist, and that's no lie!' Charles, a little embarrassed by this fulsome praise, decided it was time for business. Attempting what he thought was a conversational tone as he poured the tea, he asked 'Have you decided what you're going to do about the rowan?'

'Well now, yes I 'ave. I'm goin' to 'ave it treated. Seems only right.' The porcelain cup looked incongruous in the large calloused hands. 'After all, nobody needs to know. Nobody knows about it but you, and the bloke from the Ministry of course. And 'e don't matter.'

Charles was bemused. 'Is it important that no-one knows?' he enquired. The old man gave a snort and swallowed his tea in one gulp. 'I should think so! Don't want folks knowin' I'm daft enough to spend five 'undred pounds on a tree!'

Charles was even more bemused. 'Excuse my saying it, but if you think it's such a silly idea why are you going to do it?'

The old man shifted slightly. 'Well, - 'twas my Beth see?' Charles didn't see. "Twas 'er favourite tree,' Tom explained. 'Used to sit out under it. Allus thought it would be there like, long after we both was gone. Don't seem right somehow to let it be cut down.' Charles covered his surprise by refilling the teacups and offering the old man some cake. Finer feelings no less! He said gently 'I take it Beth was your wife?' The old man nodded assent.

'Well of course I understand your wanting to preserve the tree,' Charles said. He had to go carefully here. Perhaps the old man's change of heart was brought about by monetary considerations. Perhaps he needed financial help after all. Charles leaned forward and asked, confidentially, 'But, to put it bluntly, are you sure you can afford the expense? My offer to pay for the treatment is still open.'

He need not have worried. Tom smiled. "'Tis real good of you, and that's a fact. I'm sorry I was so short t'other day. But I 'as the money. Yes, I 'as the money.'

Charles thought a moment, and then countered. 'Even so, it's quite an expense. Perhaps you would let me contribute? Pay half each for instance.'

The old man shook his head. He looked troubled.

'Could'n do it,' he said slowly. 'I think I'd better explain, since you'm so kind.' He seemed to find it difficult. Charles waited.

'When we first moved 'ere, it was very 'ard. I worked for old man Driscoll up at the big 'ouse. I suppose we was poor, though I never thought of it that way at the time, because everybody were the same. But now I realises we was poor, no doubt about it. I did my best, and was allus in work, but the wages was low, so we never 'ad much. We 'ad a good bit to be thankful for though. Beth were a good manager, and a good mother too, when Meg came along. Yes, I couldn't 'ave 'ad a better.' He stopped for a moment, lost in memories, then continued. 'Yes, couldn't have 'ad a better. Anyway, though we managed, sometimes I used to get real fed up like. Never a penny in my pocket. I was never one for the drinkin' and suchlike, I used to bring my pay 'ome to Beth, and she would give me a bit for baccy, that's if there was enough, and she did wonders with what she 'ad, no doubt about it.'

Charles wondered if this was leading anywhere, but found himself listening intently. The old man was speaking history, with prime source knowledge of a time that was no more. Tom shifted in his seat, and continued.

'Well, I begins to cast about for ways to make a bit extra see? We was real gardeners in them days, and we used to save the seed each year in the Autumn, flowers and vegetables, to use the next Spring. We allus 'ad more seed that we could ever use, and I used to bring home any I needed. We used to grow all our own vegetables o' course, it helped a lot. Well one day when I 'ad to go into town for some supplies, I saw lots of seeds for sale at the seed merchants, and I got to wondering if 'e might buy some from me. Anyway, I went in and asked, and 'e said 'e would have a look at 'em, and if quality was good enough 'e might be interested. I didn't need tellin' twice. The next week I took 'im a fair variety of what we 'ad over, and 'e bought the lot. 'E gave me two shillin's and sixpence. Two an' six! 'Twas a fortune in them days for me!'

The old man's eyes lit up at the recollection of his triumph. Charles smiled. An entrepreneur! And in the days before it was fashionable!

'I expect Beth was pleased!'

Tom's face clouded. 'That's just it you see. I did'n tell 'er.'

'Why not?'

'I've asked myself that a 'undred times since. I don't really know. I think I just wanted to feel I 'ad a bit of money put by, a bit of my own, like. Just in case I needed it. 'Twasn't for me exactly. I never spent it. But I just liked to know I 'ad it.' He looked at Charles, a question in the look.

'I understand.' Charles was intrigued by now.

'Anyway, as time went on, each year I sold some seed and it became a nice little sideline, so to speak. My little pile of money became more and more. I used to 'ide it in an old plant pot in one of the greenhouses. Nobody ever went in there but me. But after a few years I 'ad a tidy sum, so when I went into town next time I opened an account with the Building Society. Then I used to keep the book in the plant pot. I still never told anybody. Not even Beth.'

'And this is your little nest egg? That you will use to save the tree?'

The old man nodded. 'Over the years it's amazin' 'ow it built up. There's over six 'undred pounds now. Can't think what I saved it for, seein' as I've never spent it. Never enjoyed it I mean.'

'Did you never spend any of it? Never?'

'Only once. That was when our Meg passed 'er exam to go to St. Jude's. It were the grammar school then. My Beth was that thrilled, well we both were, but the uniform cost over twenty five pounds, and we 'ad no 'ope of gettin' that. She cried that much, our Meg, 'cause she thought she could'n go! Well I 'ad a lot more than that in the Building Society by then, so I went and got twenty five pounds, and you should 'ave seen their faces when I brought it 'ome!' Tom grinned at the memory. 'I nearly told Beth then, nearly told 'er that day.'

'Why didn't you?'

'Well I enjoyed givin' 'em a surprise like. And if they knew we 'ad some money it would'n be a surprise, not ever again. And to tell the truth, I knew Beth would'n approve of me sellin' the seed. After all, weren't really my seed. Belonged to old Driscoll really. Not that e'd know, or really care. Mind, if I'd told 'im, 'e would 'ave wanted the money off me. Real old skinflint 'e was! Anyway, I told Beth and Meg as 'ow old Mr. Driscoll 'ad heerd about our Meg passin' for the big school, and asked me about it, and when I told 'im about the uniform 'e took me right in the big 'ouse and gave me twenty five pounds to pay for it. 'Course it weren't true, That old skinflint would'n give you the drippin's off 'is nose!'

The old man became thoughtful. He hesitated. Could this new found neighbour, the cello player with the posh voice and grand house, possibly understand?

'You see,' he said uncomfortably, 'Now I've lost Beth I wish I'd told 'er. It seems I kidded myself, about wantin' to surprise 'er you know. I think per'aps I was just bein' mean. Like old Driscoll. I could 'ave told 'er, but I did'n. All those years together and I never told 'er. Then when she died, - well it was too late. Did'n 'ave time. Only ill a fortnight.'

Charles was horrified to hear the break in the old man's voice. His shoulders drooped, and the lined face crumpled. 'I could 'ave bought 'er somethin' nice, - took 'er on a little 'oliday or something…'

Charles, moved in spite of himself, put a steadying hand on Tom's shoulder. 'Come on old chap, think of the tree. You can save it. You know she would have wanted that.'

Tom recovered with an effort.

'Yes, I'm sorry. It's just that I've felt so bad about things since she went. And about the money most of all.' He looked at Charles. 'You see why I've got to pay for the tree myself? And from this money?'

'Of course. But if it should prove more expensive than you thought, and you need any extra, come to see me. I'd like to save the tree for Beth, too.'

There was a silence for a few moments. There was no doubting the sense of unity which flowed between them, and yet both were also slightly embarrassed to be discussing a subject which neither hardly acknowledged as a rule. Emotion of any kind was not a luxury which Charles permitted himself, seeing it as a negation of reason. Alone, in the cocoon of his self-induced isolation, he embraced only his music and his career, and for most of the time this was enough. But the old man's story, and his belated and pathetic desire to restore his esteem with his beloved Beth, touched Charles more deeply than he would admit.

As for Tom, he went his way homeward beleaguered by a welter of emotions. He didn't know why he should have unburdened himself to Charles Erskine, of all people. He couldn't understand it, and he felt too tired to try. He walked into his tiny kitchen and sat down at the scrubbed pine table. He put his head in his hands and, for the first time since Beth died, he wept. He did not weep because she was gone, or even because of his guilt about the seed money. He wept, in great shuddering sobs, for all he had not said, all he had not done. He wept because he did not have a talent like Charles Erskine, and he wept for all the great things in the world which were denied him. He did not even know what they were. He only knew, in a hundred myriad flashes in his mind, the bitter sense of failure and defeat. At length, he dragged himself up the narrow staircase to his bedroom, and fell into a deep and dreamless sleep. When he awoke next morning, he realised to his surprise, that the great leaden lump in his chest was gone.

***

The weather seemed determined to continue fine. After a couple of wet days following Tom's visit, the clear balmy days of summer arrived and stayed almost three weeks. Charles, however, had no opportunity to enjoy the unaccustomed sunshine. After a grueling two weeks of rehearsals, and four concerts which entailed much travel, he arrived home for the weekend exhausted and moody. His reviews whilst on tour had not improved, and neither did his temper, as he recalled with some trepidation that this was the weekend when he had finally agreed that his mother should visit. He just hoped she would not be too curious, and would stay off the subject of Anna. Damn nuisance! But it had been inevitable, he could not go on putting her off for ever. Now that the time had finally arrived he began to dread it. Nevertheless he saw to the arrangements, got Mrs. Bates to prepare the spare room, ordered extra milk, and booked a good restaurant for Sunday lunch. Whilst he busied himself with these details he could avoid thinking about what he would actually say to her.

Checking his post, Charles was surprised to find four complimentary tickets for a concert at the local Town Hall on the following evening. It was to be 'an evening with our local celebrities,' and he was top of the bill! Panicking a little, he checked his diary. Damn! Yes, of course, this was the Saturday evening he had promised to do a local concert for charity. When he had invited his mother for the weekend he had completely forgotten about it. For a moment he considered cancelling, but then thought better of it. The charity organisers were sure to be badly put out if the main attraction did not turn up, they had probably sold most of their tickets on the strength of his name. There was no real problem as far as he was concerned. They would only want one fairly short piece, something well known which would not tax either him or his audience. No, the problem was his mother. Charles was well aware that there was nothing she would have enjoyed more than to accompany him to a concert, even a small local one. Charles, however, could not bear her to be there. He never allowed her to attend any of his concerts, fearing that her presence would upset his concentration. As his mind roved over the possibilities, he realised there was no getting away from her this time. Damn! At least it was just a local evening out, not a real concert. He thought for a moment of asking her not to attend, but that seemed too cruel, given her interest in and support of his career.

He wandered out onto the terrace to look around the garden, picking up Sam on his way. The cat always made a tremendous fuss when Charles returned from a tour. Charles stroked the cat absently. 'Wouldn't eat me would you?' he murmured, remembering Tom Gibsons' comment. He scrutinised the rowan carefully. It didn't look any different as far as he could see, certainly not any worse. According to Mrs. Bates men had been working on it, but he could see no obvious signs of their attentions. Remembering the old man's pleasure on hearing the cello, he decided to walk round to the cottage.

***

This time his reception was more welcoming. Tom showed him into the tiny kitchen, and insisted on making tea, talking all the time of the rowan tree, and what had been done to it since they last met. Apparently the prognosis was good, and Mr. Chalmers was satisfied, although checks would have to be carried out regularly for a while. The cozy cottage atmosphere and Tom's evident good spirits were infectious, and Charles laughed as he said: 'Spending that money seems to have agreed with you! You don't seem to be regretting it!'

'Oh no. Certainly am not. I'm much 'appier now. Now I've actually done it like, and my mind's at rest about the tree.' He shifted uncomfortably, then said with an obvious effort, "Elped me you did, you know. Oh yes. Oh yes.'

He avoided Charles' eyes as he poured the tea into large mugs, and set them down on the kitchen table. He seemed to be about to go on, and Charles waited.

"Twasn't anythin' you said like. Well at least I don't think so. Before I come to see you I'd been strugglin' with it. What to do about the tree. Knew what I should do like, but couldn't bring myself to it somehow. When I come to see you, I decided. Just made me mind up, quite easy. 'Twasn't nothin' you said. No, not what you said.' He made an effort. 'Sounds daft like, when I says it, but as soon as I heered that music, when I heered you play, I knew, I just knew what I 'ad to do.' He raised his head. 'Told you it sounded daft.'

Charles smiled. 'It's not 'daft' at all. It's well known that music can affect you, your mood, and so on. It can also help to clear the mind.' He remembered the purpose of his visit. 'By the way, as you were kind enough to say you enjoyed my playing, I wondered if you would care to come to the Town Hall tomorrow? It's a concert for charity. There will be lots of other items too. I have a spare ticket.'

The old man looked genuinely astonished. 'Well then!' he said 'That's real nice of you. I'd like to come. But if it's for charity then I should pay.'

Charles laughed. 'I daresay there will be something there you can spend your money on.' He hesitated. 'I thought if you came round at about 7 o'clock you could come with us. My mother and I. She's coming for the weekend, and so perhaps you could sit together.'

"Tis very kind of you, but I'm not much company for a lady.'

'Nonsense! You'll get on like a house on fire. Everyone gets on well with mother.' Except me, he thought bitterly.

The old man looked gratified. 'Well, if you'm sure,' he responded. 'I shall look forward to that.' He swallowed the last of his tea. 'While you'm 'ere, come and 'ave a look at the rowan.

From this side like. I'll show you my Beth's garden.' He became confidential: 'I don't show the flower garden to many.'

Charles followed him out to the garden. A heavy scent hung in the still air, and there was the sound of birdsong, lyrical but insistent. As they entered the flower garden through a rose covered archway, Charles caught his breath. At first he could only marvel at the unexpected panorama. The cottage garden was a riot of colour, with not a space between the burgeoning plants. Tall spikes of hollyhock and canterbury bells were intertwined with clematis and honeysuckle. The huge blood- red heads of peonies drooped to the carpet of forget-me-nots, pansies and violas. Roses scrambled through lupins and phlox, and the pink and white clusters of valerian. Charles eyes were drawn to one plant then another, taking in a kaleidoscope of colours and leaves, tendrils and petals. He gasped, there was too much, too much of everything, and nothing had its place. Here was no ordered harmony, but confusion and anarchy. Here the flowers fought each other for survival, vied for recognition with their gaudy colours and pungent scents. It was all alive, it almost seemed to grow as he watched it. The insistent chorus of birdsong became a raucous cacophony without meaning or harmony. It reverberated in his head. The cloying scent of the marigolds became an assault on the senses…

'Are you alright Mr. Erskine?' Charles became aware that Tom was holding his arm, looking at him anxiously.

'Yes. I'll be alright in a moment. I felt a little faint. Could we go further down? Away from the flowers?' He felt an impulse to run, but controlled it, and managed a steady walk through to the vegetable plot. Here, Charles attempted to recover his composure. The neat lines of vegetables looked well grown and healthy, and within a short time the everyday normality of the rows of onions, carrots and cabbages restored Charles' equilibrium. He turned to Tom, who was still eying him anxiously. 'I'm sorry about that,' he apologised. 'I'm a bit overwrought, I haven't had much sleep for the last two weeks. On tour, you know. You don't sleep like you do at home.'

After they had inspected the rowan, which was, Tom assured him, on its way back to recovery, they walked back to the cottage, Charles approaching the flower garden with some apprehension. But as they traversed the brick path, Charles peering right and left in spite of himself, this time he felt no menace, no threatening atmosphere. It was a dazzling cottage garden that was all, a rampant display of all that was best in English cottage gardens, overfull and overgrown perhaps, but certainly beautiful, and a paradise for the bees which hummed serenely around them. He stopped.

'Is this all your work?' he asked, not wanting to linger, but interested in spite of himself.

'Oh no. 'Twas Beth. She planted this garden, over the years. I 'elped 'er with plants sometimes, but 'tis 'er work.' Tom gazed around with satisfaction. 'I never 'ad time for flowers see. Not when I was workin'. Allus used to 'ave a good vegetable garden, but Beth did this. It was 'er specialty like. Now I just keeps it tidy for 'er. Not that it gets many weeds, no room!' He chuckled. 'It looks after itself really. Everythin' comes up each year, and lots of things sow their own seeds. Got its own life, like.'

'Yes.' said Charles faintly. 'You don't feel... well you don't feel you need to keep it under control a little more? It seems...' he fought for a word, and settled lamely on 'a bit overgrown.'

'Bless you, you can't control Nature! And you should'n try in my experience! Well only parts of it you don't like anyway. Weeds or blight or suchlike. Them you 'as to control. Otherwise it's best to let Nature 'ave 'er way, that's if you want a real garden. Often gives you lovely surprises Nature does, especially in a place like this, where it was all planned properly in the beginnin' so to speak.'

They reached the cottage. Charles was now fully recovered from his experience, and inclined to think he had imagined it. It must have been the heat, and lack of sleep. Still, he could not leave it. He turned to Tom: 'When we were out there, I thought I felt something, an atmosphere, something..., I know it seems strange, but I was, well, almost afraid.' He looked at the old man somewhat sheepishly, but Toms eyes were direct.

'Yes, I think I know what you mean. I've felt it myself sometimes. An atmosphere, yes, that's what it were, an atmosphere.' He seemed to like the unaccustomed word. 'Not afraid though, never afraid. Never felt that. Never.' He looked at Charles appraisingly. "Tis a garden planted with love, Mr. Erskine. This atmosphere you talk of... 'Tis only love. You'm not afraid of love, are you?'

***

Sleep often does not come when one needs it most. At least, that was Charles' experience, and that night was no exception. He tossed and turned, as fact and fiction became blurred in a haze of tiredness and imagination. Images of his childhood were interspersed with glimpses of concert audiences applauding. Fragments of Elgar gave way to Beethoven and then Mozart. One recurring image was the face of his father, which then blurred into his mother's face, which in turn changed into one of the big peonies from Tom Gibson's garden. Then Anna smiling at him, but her face dissolved into a jumble of flowers .... He dozed, fitfully. He was running across the sand, it was red sand, Paignton. He was a small child, dabbling in the rock pools, and measuring his tiny feet by the side of his father's large ones as they squirmed their toes around in the sand. He was trying to get into a room through a big solid door, while hushed whispers told secrets he could not understand. He could not open the door. He must get in. He must... Then hands dragged him away and he knew he would never get inside, and he was desolate, he could not bear it. He was on the sand again, but his father was not there, and he was alone, and the sand was big, and he was lost...

In the big study at school. Old Watkins. Mother in her black coat and hat, the new one. Old Watkins gloomy face as he patted him on the head. His own voice, which did not belong to him, but spun around his head in an agonised shriek. 'Don't leave me here! Mummy! Mummy! Don't leave me here!

Charles jerked awake to a sweating, palpitating awareness. God! A nightmare! He hadn't had that particular one for years. He leaned over and switched on the lamp. Three a.m. He got out of bed and walked to the bathroom, his brain still full of the images of his dream. Why should he be dreaming about his father's death now, after all these years? He'd got over all that long ago. Perhaps it was because his mother was coming tomorrow. Surely not? Surely the tensions between them could not have their roots in his childhood? Simply because she sent him away to school? What was it the old man had said? 'You'm not afraid of love, are you?'

Was he? Perhaps. After all, his experience of love, both parental and sexual, had not been what you could call encouraging. It had never actually occurred to Charles before, but there was a pattern of repeated rejections there which now struck home. God! He was becoming positively Freudian! All nonsense. He went downstairs and made coffee. No point in trying to sleep now. He'd only dream again. His mind would not clear. It was still full of images of his father and mother, school and Anna. The old man's words kept coming back to him. "'Tis only love Mr. Erskine. That's all it is.' Instinctively he reached for his cello, he would practice the piece for the charity concert. He'd give them 'The Swan.' Popular, they always liked it. With Tom's words still drumming in his head, he began to play.

***

It was almost an hour later when Charles returned to bed. After he had finished playing he had sat, pale and shaken, hardly able to bear what had just taken place. For the first time, his soul was in the music, his heart, and his heartbreak, was in the voice of the cello. Here, in the silence and privacy of his room, he had achieved a balance of technique and lyricism which he had never known before. He sat a long time, trying to make sense of his emotions, and to understand how he had interpreted these into the music. The more he analysed, the more he realised he would probably never play so well again. He did not think he could bear to reveal his emotions so openly before an audience, or indeed before himself. But when he eventually climbed the stairs, he was smiling. The Guardian critic would have loved it.

***

Tom Gibson and Marion Erskine sat together on the front row. They were in the best seats. Tom had made a real effort, and had on his best suit, which he had not worn since Meg's wedding. He could not bear to leave behind his old cap however, and he now twisted it nervously in his big hands, as they waited for Charles' appearance. They had sat through a menu of excerpts from 'The Desert Song' by the local choral society, a piano scherzo from Mrs Williams, the local piano teacher, and some really rather good renderings from Gilbert and Sullivan. Charles was last on the programme. Marion watched the old man's hands twisting at his cap. She could not imagine how Charles and he had become friends. Not that Charles was a snob, but he was so insular, so self-contained as a rule. She had noticed a difference in him this weekend however. He seemed much more relaxed, laughed more. She had noticed it the moment he opened the door, still in his dressing gown. Apparently he had overslept and had been awakened by the doorbell. Most unlike Charles to oversleep, and normally it would have put him in a bad humour for the rest of the day. But he had actually kissed her, something he hadn't done for years, and they had spent a lovely day together. He had shown her around the village, and taken her to the pub for lunch, and then had seemed to want to talk, which was very unusual for Charles. All those questions about the time his father died, and why he was sent away to school. He had always avoided these subjects in the past. And now the local concert, and this nice old man. She had liked Tom right away. Now, watching his twisting hands, she sought to put him at his ease.

'Are you enjoying it?' she asked, smiling.

'God bless you, yes! It's been really good. But I'm that nervous, now it's time for Mr. Erskine!'

Marion laughed. 'Don't worry, he won't be feeling nervous at all. He's used to much bigger halls than this. This is just like playing at home for a few friends, as far as he's concerned.'

Marion was touched. The old man seemed to have a genuine affection for her son, and this was unusual, at least since Anna. Her lips set in a firm line as she recalled Charles' behaviour at that time. Then Charles came on to the stage, and she joined in the polite applause.

From the first notes, Marion knew something was different, knew that something magical had happened to her son. The sound of the cello, vibrant and sweet, swelled with an artistry she had never heard from him before, not even in his recordings. His touch was exquisite, his musicianship superb. But it was more than that. His phrasing gave an interpretation which was moving in its majesty, sublime in its pathos. She sat entranced. She thought her heart would break.

As the last notes died away, there was a stunned silence. Then the small village hall erupted in an outburst of applause and cheering, not least from Tom, who was on his feet with the rest. Marion sat unable to speak. She had waited so long, so very long, for this moment. When at last the tumult died down she became aware of Tom. He was shaking her hands with delight and elation.

'He's a true artist, and no mistake.'

Marion swallowed. 'Yes Tom, you're right. A true artist.'

They made their way out of the hall and towards Charles' parked car. Struggling for normality, Marion asked, 'Will I be seeing you again before I go tomorrow Tom?'

Tom grinned.

'Oh yes Mrs. Erskine. I'll be around to see Charles tomorrow. His garden, well... it's a bit sparse. I've got a few cuttin's for 'im.'

THE PATIO GHOST

I looked out of the kitchen window, trying to imagine what my new patio would be like. I had imagined it many times, and so the picture came easily to my mind, and in only a week it would be a reality at last. Not that I couldn't have had it much sooner, if Gordon had just been reasonable.

'We don't need a patio there,' he would say, exasperated at my having brought the subject up yet again. 'We have a perfectly good patio right here, and plenty big enough for anything you might want to do.'

That was quite right of course, the patio ran across the back of the house, in front of the kitchen and the big doors in the lounge. The only trouble was that in the afternoon, when I might have had an hour or so to sit in the garden, it was all completely in shade, whereas that bit at the bottom, just at the end where the garage ended, always caught the afternoon sun, if there was some.

All my entreaties about the patio fell on deaf ears, and although I thought Gordon was just being bloody minded, as he held the purse strings in our house I had no alternative but to give way gracefully. I didn't forget about it though, and if I'm honest once or twice it crossed my mind that if Gordon was to go before me, (which was quite likely as he was twenty years older) I should soon see to it that I'd be sunning myself at the end of the garden, after all the ground was rough and uncultivated, and there wasn't much else you could do with it anyway.

Now, the time had come, and although Gordon's death had been a big upheaval, it was not unexpected, his fight with cancer had been a lost cause since the diagnosis. In a week I'd have my new patio, but as it was a lovely sunny day I fetched a folding chair from the garage and decided to sit out anyway. It wasn't very comfortable, but I settled down with my book in the sun. However, by the time I had found my place in the story, the wind seemed to have whipped up, and the pages of my book kept blowing over so it was almost impossible to read.

'What is this?' I said to myself, with a shiver, as the now quite sharp breeze chilled my arms. 'It's probably Gordon,' I thought. 'Wherever he is, he knows what I'm planning and is showing his disapproval.' As if to prove the point, the wind whipped sharply round the corner of the garage and I decided that for today, at least, I would read my book indoors.

As I went in I reflected that marriage to Gordon had not really turned out as I had hoped. I suppose if I'm honest I had married him because he was there, and available, and had asked me, rather than for any really deep attachment. When we met I was 24 and he was 44, and to me he seemed very worldly wise and knowledgeable, and I suppose he was. He had been married before, to a rather beautiful Indian lady named Parveen, but when they went to visit India to see her relatives, she had decided to stay behind in India, and he had come home alone, and the inevitable divorce had followed. Not that Gordon told me much about it, he was always very reticent about her, but I had heard about it from Helen, the next door neighbor, soon after I moved in with Gordon. 'Beautiful, she was', Helen had said, as if I didn't come up to scratch at all, 'And such a nice person. I have a photo somewhere…' I had pretended not to be interested, but could not help but agree when the photo eventually surfaced, a shot of Gordon and Parveen at a barbecue in Helen's back garden, both smiling and happy. Parveen was beautiful, and elegant in a yellow silk sari and with lots of gold bangles on her wrists.

After I had been married to Gordon for a few years I sometimes thought of Parveen. I wasn't surprised she had decided to stay in India, Gordon was not easy to live with. However, we rubbed along in our own fashion, and now he was gone I missed him. Well, perhaps, that's not right. I did not so much miss him, but having someone else in the house. I had never lived entirely alone before, and found it unsettling

***

The weather continued fine, and so next day I tried again to take my book outdoors. This time it was worse, the moment I went to sit in my folding chair it collapsed, sending me flying. There was nothing wrong with the chair, it had simply toppled over. 'If this is you, Gordon, 'I said, 'You'll have to try harder.' I picked up the chair and seated myself at last, but I had hardly read a page when it began to rain. 'I don't believe this,' I said as I ran for the house, 'It was a perfect day,' I went in and made myself a cup of tea, and when I looked out of the window again the rain had stopped and the little area at the end of the garage was awash with sun. Suddenly it did not seem funny any more. I have never believed in ghosts, but something, or someone, seemed intent on denying me the pleasure of sitting out beyond the garage. 'Never mind, 'I thought, the new patio will be down soon, and surely it will be fine then.'

What if it wasn't? What if every time I went out there something happened to stop me from enjoying it? If it was a ghost, or Gordon's spirit or whatever, surely he could not be so petty and unpleasant.? This was ridiculous, there were no such things as ghosts. Defiantly, I fetched my book and went out, down to the end of the garage. I stood for a moment, reflecting that it should actually be quite sheltered here, and then suddenly I got an awful feeling, which swept over me with such force that I was absolutely terrified. I had no idea what it was, but a great feeling of fear and dread engulfed me, so that I ran, literally ran, back to the house and locked the door.

When the next few days had passed, the whole thing seemed ludicrous, and as the two men arrived to build the patio I joked with them and then went in to make their first cuppa - well big mugs actually. They had been recommended by Helen, they had done a lovely patio for her a couple of years back, and she had given me their phone number and instructions on how to treat them. 'As long as you keep the tea coming every couple of hours,' she said, 'They'll do you a good job.'

I watched from the kitchen window as the kettle boiled, they were getting the drill out for the first part, where there was a concrete part. The big one was obviously in charge of that and the young lanky one with ginger hair was still bringing their stuff to the site. 'The drill makes a bit of a racket,' the big one had told me, 'But by the time you can't stand it anymore and the neighbours are thinking of complaining, it will stop. Not a big area, won't take long.'

I made the tea and then as I glanced out of the window I saw that the young lanky one was being violently sick behind the garage. What the hell...? I ran out towards them, tea forgotten. 'What's the matter with him?' I asked the big guy. The face he turned to me was white, and I followed his appalled gaze to where the drill had unearthed a skeletal arm, with many gold bangles still dangling from the wrist.

I turned away in horror as the realisation hit me, and then waited for that awful feeling of dread and fear to engulf me yet again. It did not, it had gone. Now a sense of deep calm enveloped me, and I understood. It had not been Gordon's ghost which had taunted me here, but poor, poor Parveen, who had been waiting so long for this moment.

NEW WINDOWS

Evelyn moved the fruit bowl and two silver framed photographs to create space. Then she carefully put the brochures in place, Superseal Windows on the left, Sureglaze in the middle, and the latest quote, from Decorglass, on the right. Graham had already been through the first two quotations with a fine toothcomb, and would want to compare them with the Decorglass quote, which the salesman had delivered that afternoon.

Evelyn's eyes softened, such a nice man, so polite and helpful, a caring sort of man, she thought. Of course, he was there to sell windows but still...there were salesmen, and then there were salesmen like Brian Everett...

She walked back to the dining room. Graham had finished the small cigar he allowed himself after dinner, and she began to clear the table. 'Do you want to see the Decorglass quote now?' she asked. 'It came this afternoon.'

'One thing at a time Evelyn, one thing at a time,' her husband responded, a little waspishly.

'I shall take half an hour as usual, for my digestions sake, by which time you will have finished the dishes, and can join me in consideration of all the factors involved. A joint exercise this, my dear, major expenditure, all relevant details to be examined and weighed in the balance, utmost care needed for this decision.'

'Of course dear,' Evelyn sighed as her husband made his way through to the lounge and settled in his armchair. She groaned inwardly, wondering if she would ever actually get her new windows. They had been through the whole process the year before, and after several quotes an unexpected bill for a boiler repair provoked Graham to declare that 'the window project must be shelved for a year, due to economic pressures and the appalling state of the double glazing provision in this country. Don't fret my dear,' he had admonished, 'The extra time spent waiting will allow me to become familiar with the latest building regulations with regard to the installation of replacement windows.'

It was not as though they couldn't afford it, Evelyn reasoned as she washed the dishes. There was plenty of money in the bank, they could have rebuilt the whole house if they wanted. Graham had been a good provider, she conceded, he was just so...so... She mustn't say that word, mustn't even think it. She recalled Graham's look of shock as he had responded to her outburst last week.

'What I regard as meticulous attention to detail my dear, *you* are pleased to describe as 'nit-picking!'

A little reflection and discrimination in the cool light of day will no doubt reveal to you the injustice of your use of such a word.'

She hoped that they could get it all completed before Christmas, and that nice Brian Everett from Decorglass would get the job. His were the windows she preferred anyway, although there was little to choose between them. But would it be worth it? He would no doubt be pleased with the order, but oh! to be subjected to the rigor of Graham's never ending questions, and analysis and re-analysis of the fine print in the contract. Also, she had to admit, sometimes her husband's investigations turned into castigation, and rather unpleasant sarcasm. She could not bear to think that Brian Everett might become the butt of her husband's cynicism, and she was already embarrassed that this might be the case.

Brian Everett didn't look like a salesman really, that old tweed jacket and wool tie as opposed to the business suit. Not pushy at all, and what he said about the tea, that was flattering.

'I *never* have a second cup Evelyn, but on this occasion I'll break the rule if I may, and have a top-up. Not many people know how to make a really good cup of tea.' That smile as he handed her the teacup, and those eyes, not fair for a man to have such eyelashes.

She started as her husband entered the kitchen. 'Are you ready Evelyn? Time to do battle with the double-glazing industry!'

'It's not a war, Graham,' she remonstrated. 'We're only deciding which quote to accept.'

'Every purchase a battleground Evelyn,' he countered. 'All businesses exist to maximise profits at the expense of the consumer, never forget that. Which reminds me, why are there *three* new bottles of shampoo in the bathroom cabinet? I know that is the brand you prefer, and although it costs more than we should pay for shampoo, strictly speaking, I have waived my monetary objections in deference to your preferred choice. But do you have to buy three at a time?'

'They were three for the price of two,' Evelyn said coldly. 'I only paid for two.'

'In that case I defer to your good judgment my dear,' said Graham, smiling. 'Well done, these offers can be advantageous providing of course they are only used for products one would be buying anyway. Strictly speaking of course, one should analyse the effect on cash flow of making advance purchases, but in the case of shampoo I am prepared to admit that could, just possibly, be construed as 'nit-picking."

This was quite a joke for Graham to make, and Evelyn smiled indulgently as he led the way over to the sideboard and the brochures. 'Well,' she said, 'let's take a look at Decorglass, he's left a sample of the actual window type, and a full quotation, on the whole I was very impressed. There is an extra saving if we have them installed before Christmas.'

'With all the special offers and discounts everyone claims to be making', said Graham, 'you have to remember one thing, there's no such thing as a free lunch!' He said this with great emphasis, as if it was the first time the words had been uttered. 'We shall start with A and go through to Z', he continued, 'except of course for S... I absolutely refuse to discuss soffits. Soffits are non-negotiable. I am not even going to consider soffits.'

***

A week later Evelyn and Graham discussed again the issue of replacement windows over dinner. Graham, having finally conceded that Decorglass seemed to be the best quotation, had now decided to question the standard terms and conditions of the contract.

'I don't see why one needs to put down such a large deposit,' he remonstrated. 'Realistically, we shouldn't pay a penny until the windows are installed and we are satisfied.'

'It's standard procedure now,' Evelyn said. 'All the companies ask for money up front, after all, they have to make them to measure.' Her tone was a little curt, and Graham bridled. 'I can't think why you are getting annoyed Evelyn, I'm only defending our joint interests, what is the matter with you this evening?'

'Nothing. Nothing at all.'

'Well, you are behaving in a very odd way. Putting out the best dinner service on a Wednesday, when you know it is reserved for special occasions or when we have visitors.'

'I've already explained, I just felt like using the best china...'

'And opening a bottle of wine!'

'Yes, and opening a bottle of wine, I just felt like celebrating that's all.'

'What do we have to celebrate? You are being illogical again Evelyn.'

'Well...' Her mind was racing, celebrating so much...so much...the curly hair at the nape of Brian Everett's neck, the way he had nibbled her ear...the touch of his lips...

'Well,' she said again. 'I hope we are celebrating our decision to buy our new windows from Decorglass.'

'Spending money is not a suitable matter for celebration,' Graham demurred.

'I think it's a little more than that,' said Evelyn. 'These new windows will bring a little more light into my life, and in time for Christmas too. I'm thinking of it all as a Christmas present.'

It certainly was a Christmas present, and the windows were soon installed too. All had gone well, the men had arrived on time, and had been quick and efficient. Even Graham, after endless inspections, was forced to admit a good job had been done.

After the holiday, Graham put on his raincoat as he left for his first day back at work. He turned to his wife. 'Now comes the real battle Evelyn,' he said, 'and it's one I shall have to hand over to you, as I'm so busy at the office at present. *After sales service*,' he said purposefully. 'You'll have to make sure we get the full after sales service in the New Year.'

'Don't worry dear,' she said. 'I'll make quite sure of that.'

THE BRIDE CLOTH

Madeira 1970

Jim Archer dragged himself away from the sight of a group of urchins playing football in the dusty Maderan street.

'Oh no, not again' he muttered as he saw his wife Elizabeth in deep conversation with a wiry Maderan man who was attempting to sell her some embroidered handkerchiefs. It was always the same, he thought. Wherever you went the locals heard the American accent and buzzed around like flies, trying to sell something or other. He had hoped that up in the mountains things might be different.

'Look honey…' Elizabeth turned to him, smiling. 'Not that stuff there,' she dismissed with a derisive wave a pile of lacework and embroidery which the man had stacked on a wall nearby. 'This! … Look at this!' She took a small white handkerchief from the man and held it out to him. 'Jim, honestly, in all my life I never saw work so beautiful.'

'I give way to your superior knowledge of stitchery my love.' Jim smiled at his wife; she was an expert needlewoman herself. 'But handkerchiefs? Surely no-one uses them these days… everyone uses tissues now.'

'Perhaps,' Elizabeth replied. 'But you know I'm looking for something really special for Jenny's wedding. This man's name is Paco, and he tells me his wife did this wonderful work and has other things to sell. He has invited us to go to his cottage to see them; we might just find what we're looking for…'

'Ah well, if it's for Jenny.' Jim said. He was indulgence on a plate where his daughter was concerned. 'Lead on Paco…'

Paco gathered up his piles of merchandise and led the way to his cottage where they were introduced to his wife Maria, who blushed sweetly when Elizabeth congratulated her on her handiwork. She showed them tray cloths and pillow cases, all worked with the delicacy of touch which had amazed Elizabeth.

'These are superb,' she said admiringly. 'But I really wanted something very special, as a wedding gift for my daughter, perhaps a tablecloth?'

Maria's eyes darkened and she glanced quickly at her husband. 'No,' she said defensively, 'I have nothing like that for sale.' She glanced at her husband again, and her eyes held a curious, appealing look. Paco shook his head slowly. Not a word was spoken, and yet Jim and Elizabeth felt they were watching some kind of unspoken argument. There was a palpable tension in the air which Paco finally broke.

'It is time Maria,' he said. 'Surely, it is time?' He turned to his guests. 'The truth is, my wife does have a very beautiful tablecloth, but no wish to sell it.'

'Oh….Well… May I see it at least?' Elizabeth asked. 'I am a needlewoman myself, and it would be a great privilege.'

'Well…' Maria hesitated, and then made up her mind. 'I will show,' she said, and went to a heavily carved chest, standing against the wall.

Paco went to make some tea, and Elizabeth watched as Maria carefully unwrapped the large tablecloth. She gasped in surprise as Maria spread the cloth over the table. It was the most exquisite thing she had ever seen. 'This must have taken years…' she whispered.

'Ten years,' said Maria. She smiled shyly. 'Every stitch is worked with love.' She looked into Elizabeth's eyes. 'I will tell you, for I feel you will understand. This is a bride cloth, and on the island it is the tradition that when a girl marries, she starts to make a beautiful cloth like this to give to her own daughter when she eventually marries. These flowers worked on the corners are the traditional flowers of Madeira, and they symbolise the values and gifts that a good wife brings to her marriage. This corner, the lilies, symbolise purity and virtue. The agapanthus in this corner represents generosity of spirit. The flowers of the kapok tree, which we used to collect to stuff cushions and pillows, represent industry and diligence. In the last corner is the jacaranda, which blooms in April and brings us hope and aspiration. Around the edges are the leaves of the frangipani, for this is the plant of love, which binds all together, and in the centre are the frangipani flowers, so sweetly scented and long lasting, to remind us that real love endures, and does not change with time.'

While Maria was speaking, a tear ran down her cheek. She whispered, 'My bride cloth is wasted, for I have no daughter, no children, and it is too late for me now. Paco wants to sell the bride cloth, but I think it would break my heart.'

Jim arrived with two cups of tea and said, 'Wow! That's beautiful! I'd give three hundred dollars for that!'

'No,' Paco demurred. 'The price is five hundred dollars.'

Maria burst into tears. Elizabeth felt so moved she could hardly speak, but she drew Maria aside and said gently. 'I told you already that I have a daughter. I'd like you to see her.' She took a photograph from her handbag. 'Of course, you must not sell the cloth if you do not wish to, but I would love to give Jenny this wonderful gift and explain to her the meaning of the flowers, I know the cloth would be greatly treasured.'

Maria studied the photograph carefully. 'I knew this day would come,' she said. 'You must forgive Paco if he seems mercenary, but as he gets older money seems more important to him. I forgive him, for if I have no daughter, neither does he have a son.'

She turned to Elizabeth. 'I do not want my bride cloth to moulder away,' she said. 'I would like to give it as a gift to your daughter, with my love.'

Elizabeth felt the tears sting her eyes, as the two women embraced.

Paco and Jim carried the tea cups out to the kitchen. Jim took out his cheque book.

'That's four hundred dollars then?' said Paco.

'You got a deal,' said Jim.

TURNING POINT

◆——————◆——————◆

The next day I wake up and know for certain I have really blown it. I close my eyes again and try to shut it all out. My mind seizes up and vainly I try to return to that dark recess where the world cannot intrude, and dreams drift and sway... It is no use. I am awake. For a moment I contemplate flight but realise I don't want to go anywhere. I want to stay here. Here in bed. I simply will not go into work, not ever again. Leave the boss to sort it out...

'Come on love, you'll be late!' Anna, still in her dressing gown, comes across and sits on the edge of the bed. 'I'll bet you feel awful,' she says. I try to detect hostility in her voice, after all it would be fair enough after last night, but there seems to be none as she continues softly, 'What is it Dan? What happened?'

I stare at her. She is not angry, she is worried, and that makes me feel worse. 'Nothing,' I say shortly, as I heave myself out of bed and make for the bathroom.

Over breakfast I can tell Anna is attempting to find out, trying to help without prying too much, hoping I'll volunteer some simple explanation as to why I (literally) rolled home at one a.m. last night, blabbering drunken nonsense and threatening the destruction of the universe.

I don't deserve her, I tell myself, switching off from my problems. It's pleasant, (after two Alka Seltzers have cleared some of the fog), to simply sit and watch her organise Tim and Bryony for school, doling out cereals and clean hankies, making them laugh, finding pencil boxes and fastening satchels. She glances across at me. 'It's nearly half past.'

'I know.' I say darkly.

I watch her helping Tim on with his raincoat and checking Bryony's shoelaces, and I wonder to myself, not for the first time, just what she can have ever seen in me. The children are intrigued by the change in routine, kissing Daddy goodbye and leaving him in the kitchen instead of the other way round. Anna sees them to the front door, then comes back and sits down, reaching for a piece of toast. 'Are Chalfonts closing down then?'

'Probably.' I say at length.

For the first time a note of irritation creeps into her voice. 'Dan! What do you mean... probably? Has Jack Chalfont decided to close down, or what?'

It is a reasonable question. She knows how important Westcross is to us.

'I lost the Westcross business,' I say.

'Lost it? How? You mean you lost an order?'

'No, not an order. The lot. When I called at Westcross yesterday to see their Managing Director. Geoff Collins? You've heard me speak of him? Well... we had a row, and I blew it...'

'But it can be saved surely? When you have both calmed down?'

'No. You don't understand. I lost my temper... made it personal... called him...'

God! What had I called him? Phrases like "conniving bastard" and "corrupt old scumbag" float through my mind. I smile at Anna sheepishly. 'Rest assured,' I say, 'I blew it'.

'Have you lost your job?'

It requires a 'yes' or 'no' answer. After a moment I say, 'I think so.'

'Is Chalfont's closing down then?'

'I lost my temper and it can't be repaired. No way. And we can't continue without the Westcross business, so...yes.'

Looking at her perplexed face I can see she doesn't believe me. I don't blame her, it's hardly my normal behaviour.

'Dan? What did he do? Geoff Collins? Why did you lose your temper?'

She knows me so well. Why indeed? I turn away, still wondering if could have handled it, compromised in some way as I have so many times before, adjusted my thinking as all businessmen have to do in these days of thin margins and fear of redundancies. The answer is the same. This time I could not have compromised.

'Dan?' Anna prompts.

'He wanted me to cut the quality specification on a part, so he could get it at a much lower price,' I said.

'Is that all?'

'ALL!' I round on her, my anger of last night returning. 'It's a vital part, it's crucial to *their* operation. If we compromised on quality they would have breakdowns on their production lines within months, then it would be *us* in the shit for producing faulty parts!'

My fist hits the table in my exasperation. 'Anna, the whole thing was a nonsense... it could never have worked. I couldn't believe what he was asking me to do. When I tried to explain, he actually offered me money! A bribe Anna! To push it through so that he can show better profit figures on this big order they have.' I laugh bitterly. 'I always knew Geoff Collins was a tough businessman, drives a hard bargain, but I never thought he could be ... corrupt! Apparently he's only interested in his year-end figures. He says he wants to show bigger profits this year, and will let next year and its inevitable problems, take care of themselves.'

Anna stares at me.

'Next year,' I explain patiently, 'their Chairman retires, and Geoff Collins is hoping for the job. He wants a big impression on the shareholders now, to advance his prospects. Next year when the chickens come home to roost and they are in trouble, he will blame it all on whatever poor sod takes over as M.D.'

'I see,' she says quietly, 'And so...?'

'And so I told him where to stuff his suggestions,' I tell her. 'Told him, (if I remember correctly), to stuff his inferior parts up his own inferior arse, among other things...'

'Oh dear!' As our eyes meet I see a hint of amusement there, and in spite of my worries the memory of that glorious moment tickles me, and I begin to chuckle. 'It comes to something Anna, when the *customer* actually asks the *supplier* to cut corners and supply inferior goods! If this is the business world in the new millennium, I'll be glad to be out of it.'

This time she doesn't smile with me, and the look on her face sobers me again.

'Does the boss know?' she asks.

'Not yet.' I had gone straight to the pub from Westcross, delaying the moment I had to tell Jack Chalfont I had lost our best, practically our only, customer.

'What will you tell him?'

I shrug. 'The truth, just what happened. If I survive long enough to explain, I reckon he'll understand. He's a hard man, but he's never been crooked. He was bound to retire soon anyway, and this will make the decision for him. It's the workforce I feel sorry for.'

'You'll really have to close down?'

'It's inevitable. We can't survive without Westcross business.' I look up at her anxious face. 'Sorry love, thin times ahead.'

She comes round the table and kisses me. 'Come on. If you're going to be late for the first time in nine years, best not make it more than half an hour.'

*

When I arrived at Chalfont's, Pete Shipley, the man on the gate, looks at me in surprise and then at his watch, as if he must have made a mistake.

'Morning Pete,' I say briskly, feeling for some unaccountable reason that I ought to try and explain my late arrival.

'Morning Sir,' he says, and I move on quickly across the shop floor towards the stairs, trying to avoid the surprised faces of the workforce, who know I am always there before they arrive, and long after they depart. They probably think I live here. I suddenly realise they probably know as little about me as I do about them. Pete Shipley for instance, I know he has a wife because he brought her to the Christmas dance, but does he have children? I am ashamed that I know so little about him, or most of the other men and women who stand to lose their jobs when the Westcross business goes.

My fault, all my fault.

***

'Dan! Where've you been?' Mr. Chalfont's secretary says as I walk into the inner sanctum. 'Are you alright?'

'Of course.' I say lightly. She is the third person to comment on the fact that I am late. I decide to be late more often, it seems to create a stir. That is of course if I get the opportunity, and don't get the bum's rush within the next ten minutes.

'Is he in?' I ask, nodding at Jack Chalfont's door.

'Yes.'

At that moment the door opens and Geoff Collins comes out. My fears are confirmed. It hasn't taken him long to put the boot in. Rather to my surprise he claps me on the shoulder.

'Sorry about all this Dan,' he says cheerfully, 'But all's fair in love and business.'

'Is it?' I say mechanically, seeking for some sign on the face of Jack Chalfont, who is behind him.

'Come in Dan,' he says, as Geoff Collins departs, 'Geoff is on his way to a meeting and can't join us. We did want to see you together,' he adds pointedly, 'But you're late.'

'Yes,' I agree emphatically, 'I am!'

'Anyway,' Jack continues, 'We have plenty to talk about, and that's why Geoff was here.' As we enter the office he indicates for me to sit. At least he is not red in the face with anger, in fact he seems quite cheerful as he takes his seat behind his desk. He leans towards me and says in his quietly confidential manner,

'You are the first to know, Dan. I'm selling Chalfont's. It's time for me to retire, and Westcross have made a good offer.'

'Westcross? You're selling Chalfonts to Westcross?' My mind races, trying to analyse it.

'It makes good sense,' Jack says, pouring coffee and handing me a cup. 'Geoff Collins is no fool. He knows Westcross rely on us for quality precision parts, it's vital for him to ensure continuity of supply. If we become a subsidiary of Westcross they protect their future.'

'I can see that,' I say, warily.

Jack makes his hands into a steeple. 'Dan, I want you to know I have recommended you to run Chalfonts for them. You know the business inside out and you've earned it. You will be the new Managing Director of Chalfonts, responsible to Geoff Collins.'

'What?' I am tongue-tied. Surely Geoff Collins wouldn't buy up the company as a way of controlling me? It's nonsense...

'Congratulations Dan,' Jack is saying. 'Geoff came in this morning to tell me his decision. I recommended you weeks ago, but he's only just made up his mind. He eyes me narrowly, 'What happened last night?' he asks.

'Happened? Er... what do you mean?' I stammer.

'He told me this morning he has always known how good you were at your job, efficient, and hard working... all of that. But he didn't really know you well, had a suspicion you might be a bit of a 'yes' man. He said last night was a turning point. Said he gave you some sort of test. Apparently you came through with flying colours.'

BEST SERVED COLD

It was as if the mighty power of an electric shock had hit Sophie in the solar plexus, with all its appalling force. It wasn't painful, at least not physically, but when she put down the phone she was almost paralysed with shock. It was as if some huge monster had suddenly swept her up, jangled her about in its dreadful jaws, and then crunched her into pieces before it spat her out to where she now stood, staring at the phone, fearful and disorientated.

When, a few cups of strong coffee later, she managed to think about Peter's phone call with at least some measure of rationality, she realised that, of course, she should have seen it coming.

A few small things had been different the last time he was home. And she now saw they were perhaps pointers to the break-up of their relationship, which she would have noticed if she had been more alert and less in love. Peter had been in London for only a week during the last month, and on two evenings of that week he had arrived home very late, pleading long meetings. She now reflected that that wouldn't have happened a year ago, when he could hardly wait to come home to her.

On one of those evenings she had prepared a special dinner, and when she complained next morning that he could at least have phoned, Peter had responded coldly that she had always known that business was first and last with him. When he had left for the airport there had been an atmosphere, not exactly of animosity, but certainly lacking the passionate intensity of past goodbyes. She had thought at the time they were perhaps at last settling down, becoming like a long-married couple, (although of course they were not married), and the thought had given her an odd feeling, a combination of resignation and comfortable security. She had been wrong to feel that! Oh...so wrong! And yet, until today, Peter had not said anything to indicate he was unhappy or dissatisfied in any way, but now this sudden phone call, so cold, so disinterested...how could he do this to her?

A few phrases imposed themselves again and again into her tortured mind... 'It's just not working any more Sophie'....'Far East for six weeks, plenty of time for you to find somewhere else,' .... 'Grateful for the past year....' *as if she was some kind of employee being given her marching orders.*

***

She stared gloomily around, and even now, yes, even when she was feeling at her worst, the elegant room soothed her, surrounding her with its opulent warmth and comfort. She loved the apartment, with its prime location in Mayfair and its beautiful views, and during the year since she had moved in with Peter Grant she had cared for it lovingly. Knowing how much Peter valued its priceless contents, she had embraced them too, and had spent many happy hours carefully dusting the treasures, cherishing the beautiful antique furniture and polishing the silver and crystal, until each lovely piece was a valued friend.

Peter's finest possession was the priceless Aubusson carpet, which had been in his family for generations, having been woven to a special design for what had been the Grant family seat in Oxfordshire. After years of his ancestor's profligacy and mismanagement, Peter's father had eventually been forced to sell the whole estate to pay off ever mounting debts. Peter had rescued the Aubusson carpet and a few other treasures, and they had become the foundation for his fight back to financial security and acceptance once again. She recalled Peter's words when he explained to her about not walking on the carpet wearing shoes. *'This Aubusson carpet is me....it is all I am and all I hope to be....'*

Sophie had felt at the time that Peter's was an understandable passion, the carpet was symbolic of his rather endearing desire to restore his family's name and position in life. He had certainly succeeded as far as money was concerned, he was extremely rich, just how rich, she had no idea.

And the carpet was a lovely thing. Sophie knelt down and lovingly traced the design with her fingers, delighting in its silky softness and the delicate hues of pinks, creams and blues....

The phone rang and her heart missed a beat. It was a mistake. He didn't mean it.

It was Betty, Peter's secretary, exuding a mixture of sympathy and quiet efficiency. 'Mr Grant has told me you will be leaving the flat, this is just to let you know I am here to help, if you should need any assistance or have any problems or queries....'

Helping to ease me out gently, *Sophie thought bitterly*. Making sure I don't cause any trouble.

'I can put you in touch with a good accommodation agency if you wish,' Betty was continuing. 'It's not easy now in London but Mr Grant's name can always pull a few strings.'

'That won't be necessary,' Sophie managed to say with some degree of normality, 'I shall go to stay with my aunt for a while...'

Now where had that come from? Somewhere, deep inside, was the sure knowledge that Aunt Bessie was always there, in her cluttered cottage with the heavenly garden. Aunt Bessie, warmth and love and rhubarb pie....

'Oh, that sounds lovely! So nice to be able to spend time with your family.' Betty's enthusiasm was obviously born of relief, and it occurred to Sophie that this had happened before. Had Betty had to deal with Peter's previous cast-off lovers? Had she been the one to placate crying women after Peter moved on?

'No problem at all,' she assured Betty. 'I'll be moving out once I've arranged everything.'

'Mr Grant won't be back until the 26th of next month,' Betty said. 'So you've plenty of time to organise yourself, over six weeks, but do let me know if I can help.'

Sophie put down the phone and gazed around the apartment. When she looked at it objectively, there was little of herself here. That big plant in the hall, that was about it, together with her books and clothes, some music and bits and pieces from the bedroom. She remembered buying the plant, thinking it would soften a dark corner of the living room, but Peter had objected. *'I hate plants cluttering the place,'* he had said. *'Not here, not with my favourite things.'*

'But I love it!' Sophie had remonstrated.

'Well...perhaps put it in the hall...' Peter had compromised, though not with enthusiasm.

And in the hall it had stayed, and Sophie's love of plants was not encouraged. 'I don't mind flowers...' *Peter had said.* 'An arrangement, properly done of course. But no pot plants. Please...spare me from pot plants!'

Sophie's interest in and love for growing things had therefore been put aside, as indeed she had put aside so much when Peter came into her life, even her job. Not that it was much of a job, she thought now. It had seemed illogical to continue working in an Estate Agent's office for subsistence pay, when Peter offered the alternative of moving in with him. She could live in luxury with her days free to read and meet friends, she could live as she wished provided she took care of the flat and was there when Peter came home. Had it been as mercenary as that? she wondered for the first time. Had she moved in with Peter Grant because he offered her an easy and luxurious life style? Was that really all it was? In her heart she knew this was not the case, she loved him, really loved him. She loved his looks, his easy grace, his conversation and his cleverness, she loved to be with him and during the past year she had counted the days until he returned from his many trips abroad. She loved him, no matter what he had done, and you could not stop loving someone just because they had stopped loving you.

She picked up the phone and dialled the Company's number, and was put through to Betty.

'I wonder if you can tell me where Peter...er...Mr Grant is today? Perhaps you have a contact phone number?'

'I'm afraid not,' Betty's tone was solicitous but firm. 'Mr Grant cannot be contacted today.'

'Well, where will he be tomorrow? Surely you know that?'

'If I do,' Betty responded, 'You will understand I am under strict instructions not to reveal it.'

'To me, you mean?'

'I'm sorry Sophie, but as I explained, if you have any queries Mr Grant would prefer me to deal with them for him.'

'I'll bet!' Sophie said bitterly as she put down the phone. Aloud she said, 'How do you deal with this Betty? Is a broken heart mended by helping me find a new flat or a new job? Can Peter really buy everything, really everything, with money and influence?'

That evening, alone in the apartment, she lurched between bouts of tearful despair at her loss, and anger at the way she had been treated. She switched on the television, but even Alan Titchmarsh explaining how to seed a perfect lawn did not cheer her. In desperation she rang her closest friend and arranged to meet next day for lunch.

***

'Sue the rotten bugger,' said Mary, when a sniffling Sophie had explained the situation. 'Take him for all you can, he's worth millions...'

'Sue him for *what* exactly?' Sophie opined. 'Breach of promise? He never promised me anything, and anyway, you can't these days, at least I don't think you can.'

'Well make him pay in some way...' Mary was furious.

'I don't want him to pay, I don't want his money, I never did... I just want...' Sophie wiped her eyes. 'I'm just so hurt that's all, he didn't even tell me face to face. Just a phone call...and it's all over.'

'Well he's a cowardly bastard!' Mary said. 'Why don't you cut up all his suits like that woman in the paper?'

'What would be the point of that? He'd only replace them right away.'

Nevertheless, Sophie smiled in spite of herself. Mary's anger was infectious, and she was warming to her theme: 'Trash his flat, put sugar in the central heating pump, break his car windows, spread vicious stories about him, but for God's sake do *something* ... if only to make you feel better.'

Sophie was almost laughing now. 'Stop! I couldn't do anything like that, I'm simply not the type... You can't take your feelings out on inanimate objects, it doesn't work, and none of that would really upset him. I suppose,' she said sadly, 'You can't blame someone for falling out of love with you.'

'Perhaps not,' said Mary. 'But you *can* blame him for being such an insensitive prat...and for not even talking it over. Don't worry love, we'll get through the next few weeks, and then Peter Grant will be just a bad memory.'

Mary was as good as her word, and proved a staunch friend over the next few weeks, as Sophie began to come to terms with her new situation. She wrote to Aunt Bessie, who was delighted at the prospect of having her niece to stay, and then spent her days between boozy lunches with Mary, and visits to the local garden centre.

As the 26th approached Sophie began to pack up the few personal items she had brought to the flat, together with her books, music and clothes. She was determined not to move out until the 26th, the day when Peter was returning home, and on that morning, as she was putting her suitcases in the hall, the phone rang. It was Betty.

'Oh Sophie!' she sounded displeased. 'I was just checking. I thought you would be gone by now.'

'I'm just leaving,' Sophie said. 'I've already rung for a taxi to take me and my last suitcases.'

'Oh good,' Betty sounded relieved, but added, 'Of course, you know they'll be home this evening so you really mustn't be there.'

Sophie had not missed the reference to 'they.'

'No problem,' she said calmly. 'I'm catching the train to my aunt's this afternoon.'

'Oh fine. Do have a good stay with your aunt, I think you had better give me the telephone number.'

'I'm sorry Betty, that's not possible. Like Mr Grant, from today I'm not contactable.'

Sophie put down the phone and regarded the living room with satisfaction. She walked carefully around the Aubusson carpet, treading on the parquet surround as she was wearing her outdoor shoes. At the doorway she stopped, allowing her eyes to sweep over the new lawn. It gave the room a whole new perspective. Alan Titchmarsh was right, you could create a perfect lawn in six weeks. The Aubusson carpet, heavily watered and then thickly spread with rich, dark compost, was a perfect bed on which the lawn seed had readily sprouted. She had turned up the central heating to speed germination, and had quickly re-seeded any patchy areas to ensure a thick green sward. Regular watering over the six weeks had produced a lawn to be proud of.

The taxi was here. Sophie picked up her suitcases and let herself out of the flat, closing the door behind her and pushing the keys through the letterbox. 'Oh dear,' she reflected as she walked to the lift, 'I don't think Peter has a lawnmower...'

SUMMER DESTINY

When Roz decided to take her sandwiches to the park to eat, rather than face the crowded bus home and her empty flat, she could hardly have expected to find it there. Her destiny that is, or what could pass for destiny in her 21st century world of ever more regulation and conformity, and her own unquestioning acceptance of the routine and daily rigours of office life.

She had pondered often lately upon the question of her destiny. It had seemed to her that she was simply marking time with her job at the insurance office and her unremarkable life. She had a job, and friends, and a small flat, but that was it. What was her place in the world? What was she going to do to astound everyone? Or at least make some impression? She must have some kind of destiny, something awaiting her? Today the questions resounded with a new relevance in the warm air. After the freezing winter and a cold, blowy spring, the glorious sun seemed to herald a wonderful feeling of hope. On a day like this, she thought, with the hot summer sunshine permeating her cotton dress to warm and melt body and soul, anything was possible.

It had been several months since she had made the conscious decision that it was time to have an affair. There had been no-one since Tim, and although she had no wish to repeat that sorry episode, it was time to move on. Time now surely, for her to emerge from her self – imposed chrysalis and sample the delights of modern living. Other people had full lives; why should she be different? Yes, it was time, time for passion and new experiences, time for change, a new love, a new life, and today the balmy summer afternoon added poignant urgency to her imagined re-birth.

Making her decision had been one thing, implementing it was quite another. Eligible *'homo sapiens'* were very thin on the ground. She needed nothing superhuman, just a kind man, caring and gentle and without an over inflated ego, who would let her be herself and love her in spite of her gammy leg and fine hair which needed washing every day. Joining the Ramblers club and the local History Society had provided no such paragon. Her dream had faded, and on that lovely summer day in the park, nothing was further from her mind as she sat on a bench and opened her sandwiches. Then, quite suddenly, she saw him.

He was walking towards her and smiled, an easy 'Good afternoon' type of smile, and she knew, instantaneously she *knew*, that even if he was not the man, he was certainly the *kind* of man, who would be her destiny.

In sudden agitation she dropped her sandwich wrapper, which fluttered away on the breeze. Mr Destiny chased it, lost it, chased it again and caught it, bringing it back to her, laughing and breathless, offering it like a gift.

'Caught it,' he said. 'I wish I could do that at cricket.' He smiled. 'Do you need this?' His laughing eyes regarded her with intense interest.

'Oh no...er...no, thank you. It's only the bag from my sandwiches, but I hate litter don't you?'

Roz watched him as he deposited the bag in a nearby litter bin, together with another he had found on the way. He came back and sat on the bench beside her, still smiling. 'We all feel so guilty about litter these days, don't we?'

'Yes, but I admit I am a bit keen on protecting the environment. Would you like a sandwich? They're cheese and beetroot.'

And so it began. By the time the sun had lowered to a glorious orange and grey dusk, they were bosom friends, talking instinctively without barriers, warming to each other's anecdotes, sharing small secrets and making each other laugh.

As they left the park he took her arm protectively and said 'You know, it seems strange, but I don't know your name.'

'It's Roz, short for Roseanna.' She laughed, exhilarated, alive. It was happening, coming true.

The kind eyes were warm. 'And I'm Joseph. Joe if you like. Joe Beddows. Shall we go?'

***

The Detective Superintendent looked away. He had seen enough.

'Why?' he muttered. 'Why do they do it?' he turned to his sergeant in exasperation. 'Tell me Jim, what makes a normal, decent young woman invite a complete stranger to her flat?'

'God knows,' the sergeant said. 'Perhaps it was this hot spell. It's amazing how a bit of sun can make people do stupid things. It must addle their brains...' He broke off as the phone rang. He picked it up and after a short conversation turned to his boss. 'Good news sir, we've got Beddows. Picked him up an hour ago, he's already on his way back to Broadmoor, thank God. We can interview him there when we are ready.'

***

Three months later, a bored police clerk on filing duty slid a thick elastic band around the folder marked 'Roseanna Nash'. Even in these days of computers, she thought, there was still plenty of paperwork.

On her way downstairs, she stopped at the coffee machine and filled a white plastic beaker, before descending further to the Records section. Hesitating only a moment, she made her way to the Homicide shelf. Feeling her way alphabetically along the row, she filed the folder marked 'Roseanna Nash' next to one marked 'Nameless.'

Roz had found her destiny.

RESOLUTION

I had waited sixty years, and then, quite suddenly, he was there. My heart lurched and my mouth went dry. I told myself my senses were deceiving me, but there was no mistake, this time it was true. As he stopped at the hotel reception desk to order coffee, there was, in spite of his age, something about his bearing and manner which was instantly recognisable to me.

As he turned towards me to take a seat in the lounge, I stood up and made my way to the lift, leaning heavily on the crutch which has supported my left side since my stroke six months ago. My heart was racing now and my feet felt like lead, and all I wanted to do was run…...

In the lift, my heart still pounding, I willed the agonisingly slow steel doors to close, close me in, make me safe.

In my room at last, the door locked behind me, I leaned against the wall, and they were there with me, the little girl with the big eyes clutching her rag doll, the confused old man holding grimly onto a piece of cloth, and young Mrs Hertzman, pregnant and anxious, who kept asking 'Why am I here?'

It is strange that from the thousands of memories which must be stored in my mind, these three are those which arise most often. Perhaps they are the pivotal moments, those which help to make us what we are. All I know is that these people are my friends, as dear to me as my own family.

I went out on the balcony and breathed in the sweet fresh air. As I gazed at the familiar view of the lake, bordered by grassy slopes and distant mountains, I was deeply ashamed. I had always expected to feel anger and revulsion, but all I had felt was fear.

There was no logic to it, only the pure emotion of blind terror which had lain inside me for sixty years, and which I thought had been subdued. I was still so afraid of him, afraid of Kessler.

My immediate instinct was to ring my daughter Helena. She was the only one who understood the reason I came to this small village near Lugano every year in April. I *knew*, that some day Kessler would appear. I had heard him boast many times that his favourite place in all the world was this little village of Eigenstadt, where he went every April to sample the best coffee and strudel imaginable at the village inn.

I dismissed the idea of telephoning Helena. If she knew Kessler had actually turned up she would be on the next plane. This was something I must deal with, provided I could get over this irrational fear. There was nothing to be afraid of, Kessler was even older than me. Of course, I understood why he had come. I had always known that with increasing age he would need to see Eigenstadt again, just once.

I gathered my courage; I now had to put my long planned deceit into action. I made my way downstairs to reception. I glanced across to where Kessler was just finishing a cream cake with his coffee. No change there then. I could still see him stuffing the special cream cakes which were made for him by his personal cook, and were brought to him as he supervised the selections for work details. I banished the memory, action was needed now. I smiled at the young receptionist. 'Could you please do me a great favour?'

Only minutes later, I used blu-tack to stick up notices in each of the four hotel lifts. They read:

Chess Partner wanted.

Please ring room 126

Günter Strauss.

I had asked for the notices to be printed in German and English, hoping Kessler would rise to the bait. I was due to leave the hotel in three days time, and had no idea how to proceed if the chess gambit failed. In the camp he had been very proud of his ability to beat his colleagues, who were told to look out for any prisoner who could play chess well. One old Jewish gentleman had delayed his own death for almost six months, by being able to provide Kessler with a decent game. Years later I learned chess myself, and Helena and I played regularly.

That evening I had two phone calls. One was from an American, whom I agreed to play at eleven the following morning, and the other was someone who said his name was Heinrich Dorn. I could tell from the timbre of his voice that this was indeed Kessler, no matter what he now called himself. I arranged to play him in the lounge at two o'clock in the afternoon.

The American was young and eager and insisted on calling me 'Sir.' These college graduates always impress me with their intelligence and good manners. I looked at him, frowning with intensity over the board, and loved him for that other one, who stroked my head and kept saying 'O.K. now buddy, a little at a time,' as he spooned soup into my mouth.

This young fellow had not been playing long, and I beat him easily. He took it with good grace and said it was an honour to lose to a master! Yes, of course I enjoyed it, but realised that beating Kessler would not be so easy.

At two o'clock that afternoon, I watched him approach me in the lounge. He was perfectly dressed and still ramrod straight, but he walked with a hesitant gait and with age had lost much weight, so that he looked gaunt and haggard. *Not much chance of him coming to trial*, I thought, even if I had the stamina needed to expose him.

'Günter Strauss?' he enquired pleasantly.

'Yes,' I answered, rising to take his hand.

'I thought it must be you,' he said, settling himself into the armchair opposite. 'I saw you playing that American boy this morning. Did you beat him?'

'Yes,' I said, 'But he hasn't been playing long, he has promise, I'm sure.'

It was surreal. I was holding a normal conversation with him, when for sixty years I had dreamed of cutting his throat.

'Well, shall we begin?' he said politely. 'I am not as good a player now as I was, my memory lets me down, I am eighty five you know.' He said this with pride, as if it was some sort of achievement, and given the circumstances I suppose that it was.

'Shall we have some wine to help us along?' I asked. 'Or perhaps you would prefer a brandy?'

'A brandy would be perfect,' he said. 'I have a heart condition you know.'

Good, I said to myself as I walked to the bar, still wondering if this was really happening. When I returned he had the board set up.

'Shall we toss for black and white?' I said.

'Black,' he said firmly. 'I always play black, unless you have an objection?'

'Of course not,' I said easily, and made my opening move.

***

By the time we finished the game I realised he was not the man he once was. He was not able to visualise even a few moves ahead, with the result that I beat him, not easily, but without too much difficulty. 'It's my age,' he said, annoyed with himself, 'I shall have to stop playing.'

'Does that mean you can only enjoy it when you win?' I said, and immediately regretted it. I did not want to put him on his guard. He seemed not to have noticed my implied criticism however and said, 'Of course I like to win, doesn't everybody?'

'I'm sure they do,' I said. 'Thank you for the game. Will you join me for a short walk into the village? I usually have a walk in the afternoon.'

'Yes. I should like that,' he said, and we left the hotel together, two old fogeys creaking along at a necessarily slow pace.

What next? I was perplexed. Playing chess with the old man had made me unsure of my motives. What did I want from Kessler? An acknowledgement of who he was and what he had been? Unlikely, and anyway I didn't need it. I knew who he was and what he had been.

As we crossed the road from the hotel, it occurred to me I could perhaps push him under a car or bus, but there was nothing coming. We crossed in safety and began to walk along the path which bordered the lake.

'Lovely spot isn't it?' I said, for something to say.

'Yes, but it has changed a lot,' he said.

'Really?'

'Yes, of course. I used to come here every year, before the war you know. It was quite remote then. Our hotel was just the village inn then, it was a perfect place.'

'I'm sure it was,' I said, 'but admit it Heinrich, the rooms were not so warm and comfortable, and it certainly wouldn't have had the indoor heated pool, or the TV for when it rains.'

He smiled. 'Of course. Different times. I will have to try the pool, I still swim a little.' We had stopped at an elevated part of the path, where there was a steep drop to the lake below. For a wild moment I contemplated trying to tip him over the small rail, but realised I probably didn't have the strength.

What did I want from him? Justice? No, that was impossible for the little girl with the big eyes and the rag doll, for young Mrs. Hertzman and the confused old man with his piece of cloth. It was too late for justice.

Revenge then, it was pure revenge that I wanted, but I did not believe in revenge. But for Kessler? One thing had certainly happened; my terror of him had gone. He no longer held the whip hand; he had no power over me now. He was a frail old man, that was all.

As we returned to the hotel, we passed a young dropout, who had settled himself into the shelter of a kiosk, not yet open for the summer trade. He held out his hand as we passed, and Kessler said, 'Layabout! There is so much of it these days!' He leaned towards me confidentially. 'Say what you like Günter, in our day we knew how to deal with the dross.'

I felt a shard of ice go through me.

'You think so?' I said, with as little emphasis as I could.

'Of course. There were bad times of course, you're only a few years younger than me, I'm sure you will agree there were bad times.'

'Oh yes,' I said. 'I had bad times.'

'Ah!' he said. 'Of course, the bombing, that was terrible. How we suffered in the bombing! But for all that, you would not have seen a young man begging in the street like that!'

'No,' I said. 'You probably wouldn't.'

'Dross!' he said. 'Just dross! They need regulation, the youth today. Discipline, and something to aim for…'

Like the Hitler youth, I thought, as we entered the hotel.

***

By the following afternoon I was reconciled to the idea that nothing could happen.

I had spent a restless night trying to work out a plan, to no avail. I had got to know him, but now doubted my own motives and my ability to act.

At three in the afternoon I made my way down to the hotel's indoor swimming pool. It was a small, kidney shaped pool, not large enough for the serious swimmer but ideal for holiday makers. A draught of warm moist air greeted me as I entered the pool area, and I was surprised to see Kessler in the pool, along with an Italian woman and her family, who were making a great deal of noise. I gave Kessler a wave, and he nodded and smiled. I went over to one of the sun beds and took off my cardigan. Then something happened which you may call Fate, or Providence, but as far as I was concerned it was a miracle. The Italian mama called her brood to order, put towels around them, and marched them off. They went with shouts and giggles and calls for ice cream, and quite suddenly there was only Kessler and myself, and silence, and the warm inviting pool.

He surfaced at the far end, and I said, 'It's gone quiet!'

'Yes,' he said. 'The dross is gone at last.'

I don't know if it was that word 'dross' again which was the turning point, or if it was because the opportunity was suddenly there, but I was able to act at last. As Kessler made his way up the pool towards me, showing off a little by swimming under water, I took my crutch and turned it upside down. As his head reached the end of the pool just below me, I bent down and put the round part, which normally slips over my arm, down over his scrawny neck and pushed down. He struggled, and I was surprised at his strength, but I pushed down on the crutch and held him there, under the water. I suddenly realised I had forgotten the most important part. With a heave on the crutch, I lifted his head out of the water. He was gasping, spluttering, staring at me with half glazed eyes. I held him there, with my left hand holding the crutch while I pointed with my right to the six figure number tattooed on my left wrist, the one I had refused to have removed, despite Helena's pleadings.

He understood at last, and gasped out 'But you're German!'

'Yes,' I said, and saw his look which said 'You must have done something...'

'I helped my friends!' I said. 'I was nineteen! I hid my Jewish friends!'

His eyebrows went up, as if to say 'Then what did you expect?'

I pushed down on the crutch again and his head went under, but the struggles were weaker now, and I just held on and pushed and pushed, and they were there with me, the little girl and her rag doll, anxious Mrs. Hertzman, and the confused old man with his piece of cloth, and we pushed together until all resistance was gone and the water became calm.

I retrieved the crutch and dried it with my towel. No-one had come into the pool area. I put on my cardigan and went out and along to the bar, where I ordered a gin and tonic.

As I sipped my drink in the hotel lounge, I decided not to return to Eigenstadt again. Despite all my years of holidays here, I've never really liked the place. I have an urge to see Venice again, once more, before I die.

WITHOUT A FLAW

'Stop! Oh David, stop!'

I glanced across at him. His face was white and set, but he accelerated even more and swung the car around the next bend, the headlights picking out glimpses of hedgerows and fields.

'David stop! You must stop! We hit someone!'

'We didn't hit anything,' David said through gritted teeth. He slowed a little as we went through a small village. 'Stop making such a fuss. You're becoming hysterical!'

'It was an old man, on a bike! You must have seen him, you must have felt it!'

'I didn't see anything. I felt a small bump that's all. If we hit something it must have been a fox, or a rabbit perhaps...'

'No! It was that old man, he had a grey cap on, you must have seen him, you *must*...' My voice faltered away as I realised that of course David had seen him, was fully aware of what had happened, and had no intention of stopping.

David slowed the car to normal speed, and we did not speak again until he pulled up on the drive of my parent's home. I felt slightly sick, and watched in dazed revulsion as David got out and inspected the front nearside bumper. He got back into the car. 'There is a bit of a dent,' he admitted. 'And the headlamp is cracked. I'll get it fixed tomorrow, I'm going in to Norwich for the day. I know a small garage there, a decent chap, he'll get it done for me pretty quickly I expect.'

I stared at him. 'David, we could have killed him. He could be lying there injured, we should call an ambulance.'

'Don't start that again.' David's voice was calm. He took my hand and held it. 'Look,' he said, 'whatever happened back there... have you thought it through? Have you thought what would happen if he is badly injured? If he dies?' He stroked my hand as if willing me to agree with him. 'You know if I get any more points on my licence I'll be banned from driving. If I can't drive I'll lose my job. Lose everything! Think of the house, we wouldn't get the mortgage we need... imagine! Me without a job!'

He hit the steering wheel with the palm of his hand. 'Trust something like this to happen,' he said. 'only weeks before the wedding! I can't believe it! After all my work...'

He looked at my face. 'Darling I know how you feel, I'm upset too. I'd give anything for it not to have happened, but it really wasn't my fault...'

'You were driving too fast. You always drive too fast...'

'But he came from nowhere! It was an accident, you know it was! But if the police find out they'll throw the book at me, and then where shall we be? It will affect us both you know, the wedding only three weeks away, and the house, your parents, MY parents for God's sake!... you know what the old man's like!' David kissed my fingers. 'There's no need for anyone to know,' he said. 'I'm sure we weren't seen. You won't say anything will you? I mean to your parents, or... or... anyone?' He shrugged ruefully. 'Anyway, it's a bit late now isn't it?'

A beam of light lit up the drive as my father opened the front door. He came out and walked up to the car. 'Are you ever coming in?' he said. 'Don't feel you have to snog out here, the front room's empty and it's warmer!'

I smiled at him and said, 'I'm just coming Dad, we're only talking.'

'Aren't you coming in David?'

'No,' I answered for him. 'David has an early start tomorrow, going in to Norwich.'

***

In my room I sat down at the dressing table and stared into the mirror. My white face stared back at me like a rebuke. I could hardly believe it had happened. Even harder to understand was David's reaction. We should have stopped. I looked at the telephone, waiting quietly on my bedside table. Was it too late now? Would it make matters worse if I reported it now?

I had been so happy when we set out that evening for dinner with friends. It was a lovely evening, good food, stimulating conversation and a great deal of laughter, and we had left in a convivial mood. We had enjoyed some wine, but David certainly wasn't drunk, well, not so you would notice. Even so, I thought guiltily, if he wasn't actually over the limit he must have been near it.

He was right of course. If this was a serious accident, and in my heart I knew it was, there was no doubt David would lose his license with all the consequences he had foreseen. David had made such a difference to my life. Nearing thirty, I was beginning to wonder if the path of marriage and family was closed to me. I had had a couple of early skirmishes with boyfriends who didn't last, but when David came along everything seemed to fall into place. He was good looking and kind, and the sort of person who could make any party go with a swing. All my friends liked him, even Mum and Dad liked him! 'A bit too much money for his own good, but a nice enough chap for all that,' was Dad's comment.

I looked down at the huge square cut diamond on my finger. You had to have serious money to lash out on a stone like that. I took off the ring and stared into its secret depths.

'A completely flawless stone,' the jeweller had said, on that magical day when we had stood together in his shop, making our selection. 'Most diamonds have some small flaw, sometimes several, it is in the nature of things. Undetectable to the eye of course, but there all the same. This stone is without flaw, most unusual in a diamond of this size...' He wittered on about cutting and carats and facets, and David seemed to be delighted to be parting with an extraordinary amount of money.

'A flawless stone, I like that,' he said, putting the ring on my finger. 'A flawless stone for a flawless beauty.' You can say that for David, he always has the right phrase and is never stingy with money.

I spent a sleepless night, and next day David phoned me at the office at about 3 o'clock. He didn't beat about the bush. 'No problems,' he said right away. 'I got the car in first thing and it will be done for tomorrow, they couldn't do it in the one day because the wing has to be re-sprayed, but he'll do it overnight.'

'Right.' I said dully.

'So could you pick me up from the office in Norwich later and drop me home?' he said. 'I did remember it right, you are going in to Norwich this afternoon?'

'Yes,' I said. 'It's the final fitting for my wedding dress. I'm leaving work early to go in. My appointment is at four fifteen, I'll probably be free just after 5 o'clock.'

'Perfect,' he said. 'I'll see you then.'

'David,' I said urgently.

'Yes?'

'It was on the lunch time news.'

'I know. Don't think about it.'

'I can't help it!' My voice dropped to a whisper. 'Apparently he was found over 100 yards away from his bike, he was trying to crawl for help...'

'I know.' David's voice had a hard edge, and a slight irritation was audible. 'Darling, forget it. It didn't happen. End of story. Now perk up and go and try on your beautiful wedding dress.' He paused, and then in a softer tone, 'We have so much to look forward to, remember I love you very much. See you later.'

***

Jeanette's fingers flitted like birds between the pin box and my waist.

'It'll have to be taken in another half inch,' she said. 'Are you sure you haven't been dieting?'

'No,' I said truthfully.

'It's probably the stress of it all.' Jeanette stood back and surveyed me. 'It's wonderful. I'm glad you close this one.' She looked at me dubiously. 'You are pleased with the dress aren't you? You seem a little down today.'

Bless her, she is such a kind soul, and a top seamstress too. I smiled.

'Of course, I love it,' I said. 'You have done a wonderful job.'

'That's good.' Jeanette sounded relieved. 'What is it then? I can tell you are worried about something.'

'It's just...' I hesitated. 'It's my ring.'

'Your ring?' Jeanette looked incredulous. 'Your beautiful solitaire?' She took my hand and lifted it, examining it closely.

'Yes,' I said slowly. 'The jeweller said it was a stone without a flaw, a perfect diamond. But it has a flaw. It is a dark, corrupt flaw at its very core, and I have to return it tonight.'

MICHAEL

―――♦―――

It's not often that I wake up bearing a grudge; I'm too long in the tooth for that sort of nonsense. Well, not a grudge exactly, just a vague sense of annoyance at the world in general and the local shop in particular.

Of course, it wasn't their fault that the day before I had left half my shopping behind and had to go back for it, it was just the attitude. That Myra with the spindly legs, she does everything so fast she gets me flustered.

'Forgot this bag didn't you Mrs Jackson?' she said, producing it from behind the counter.

'Oh, thank you,' I said, relieved.

'Put it by for you love.' She leaned over the counter. 'Forgot your purse as well, didn't you realise? It's here, I knew you'd be back.'

I was covered in embarrassment. I knew she was being kind but it was so patronising. She was already serving the man behind me, waiting to pay for his paper, and the look that passed between them said 'Poor old thing, shouldn't be let out.'

This scene played itself back to me as soon as I opened my eyes next day, and it still rankled. I was thinking about it as I put on my dressing gown and went downstairs. Mechanically, I opened the front curtains, and noticed a white van outside next door. Must be the painters come early. Mr Mason, the landlord, had said they were starting next week. I opened the front door, and as I stooped down for the milk a young man came out of next door. (Our front doors are so close he was only a yard away.) He went to the van and unloaded a box, and as he carried it back up the path he saw me and smiled.

I said, 'If you want a kettle boiling I'll do it for you, only I think the electric's off.'

'What?' he said.

'The electricity – it's off,' I said. 'Mr Mason turned it off last week. If you want to put it back on I've got a key for the meter cupboard, it's the same as mine.' I smiled at him, he was a good looking young man. 'You'll have to put some money in though, it's a £1 coin meter, you know, with it being a rented house. I do mine monthly, direct debit…'

I was just wondering why I had volunteered him this information when he put the box down inside next door's porch, and came back to me.

'Go inside,' he said. It was not a request.

I stared at him. 'Quickly,' he ordered. Then, more gently, 'Please…Mrs…'

'Jackson,' I said, and went in. He followed me through to the kitchen, and it was only then that it occurred to me that they might not be painters at all, perhaps they were burglars! But that made no sense, the house next door was empty.

'Sorry Mrs Jackson,' he said, 'But this is police business.'

'Police?' I repeated. He did not look like a policeman, and the white van wasn't a police car.

'Undercover operation,' he said, 'And you almost blew it for us.' He smiled, and I noticed again just how handsome he was, and he had a lovely lilt to his voice, a faint Irish accent, I thought.

'My name is Michael Robinson,' he said. 'I'm on attachment to the CID at Argyle Street.' He seemed to wait for a response, so I said 'Oh, yes, I know where that is.'

'Well,' he said. 'We are on a covert surveillance operation, me and two other chaps. They're next door.' He smiled. 'We were trying to sneak in early and were hoping not to be seen, but you're obviously an early bird.'

'Oh yes,' I said. 'Surveillance? I know all about that, you see it on 'The Bill' quite often. But there's nothing here to watch surely? There's only the fence and the old people's bungalows.'

'The back,' he said, 'Across the railway line, the houses on the other side.'

'But they're miles away,' I said. 'You can't see much there, surely?'

'Not miles,' he said. 'A hundred and fifty yards perhaps. It's amazing what long distance lenses can do these days.'

'But what are you looking for?' I said, and then… 'Oh! Drugs…'

He smiled again, he really did have lovely teeth, I noticed. 'Not drugs Mrs Jackson, not to worry. This is a nice area, no problems of that kind, at least, not as far as I know.' He hesitated. 'I can't really tell you any details, except to say that we have to stay very vigilant.' He was talking like a policeman now, and I responded immediately.

'Of course,' I said, 'Just like on 'The Bill. You get to know quite a lot about how the police do things.'

'Well, our life isn't quite as exciting as 'The Bill,' he said. 'Shouldn't you be getting the kettle on Mrs Jackson? I'm sorry I spoiled your breakfast.'

'Well, stay for a cuppa Michael,' I said. 'The others can manage without you for a few minutes can't they?'

'I expect so. While I'm here, would you mind if I took a look out of your back bedroom window? We might get a better angle on the side of the house.'

'Of course,' I said. I liked Michael. He could be only in his twenties. How good it would be to have a grandson like him.

By the time he came downstairs I had the tea brewed and a pile of hot buttered toast made. We sat in the kitchen and shared it, and Michael asked me a lot about myself and my family, finally pronouncing that I must be rather lonely.

'Oh, no,' I said, 'I have lots of friends, it's just that they live rather far away, but of course, there's the phone.'

'Yes,' he said, 'But it's not the same as a visit, does no-one visit regularly?'

'Well, no,' I admitted. 'Only the milkman.' I smiled, it was easy to chat with Michael. 'Of course, my friends visit, usually in the summer, and stay a few days.'

'That must be nice for you,' he said, and seemed more relaxed. I asked him about his own family and he told me he was on secondment from Northern Ireland. 'I have some experience which is useful here,' he said. 'As I say, we have to stay vigilant, ever since the Manchester bomb.'

I froze. Terrorism! I stared at him, not comprehending. 'But the peace process – surely that's all over?'

'Well, hopefully of course,' Michael responded. 'But as I say, we have to remain vigilant, and there are other groups now.' He stopped. 'Don't worry Mrs Jackson, lots of our so called 'leads' are just dead ends.' He hesitated. 'I've already said too much. Perhaps you understand now that it's vital you don't speak of this to anyone. Not even after we're gone. Not ever.'

'Of course,' I responded warmly. I couldn't believe this. I was involved, and actively helping, in vital police work.

'You can count on me, Michael,' I said. 'I know how to keep my counsel when it really matters.'

'I'm sure you do, Mrs Jackson,' he said. Then he said something marvellous, something I'll never forget. 'You know,' he said, 'I never knew my grandparents, and it seems to me you'd make a wonderful grandma, I can talk to you so easily. Do you mind if I think of you as my gran?'

Later that day Michael popped around again for a slice of my fruit cake and a cup of tea, and over the next couple of days he visited several times and I grew to appreciate his quiet consideration and his gentle, mocking sense of humour.

'You'll have me in trouble grandma,' he said, after I'd persuaded him into my back garden to move several big stones to make a rockery. 'I'll have you know I'm supposed to be working.'

'Well just move that big one about six inches further back,' I said, 'And that'll do. I can get on with planting it up now.' Thanks to Michael the rockery was on its way and already looking good. Michael struggled with the stone and eventually I was happy.

'Come on,' I said. 'A quick cup of tea and I'll let you go. Thanks Michael, I'd never have moved them on my own.'

'No, I must go, Grandma, the lads will be complaining I'm not doing my share.'

'Only take a minute,' I said, 'And I've made a new fruit cake.'

'Grandma, you do know how to tempt a fella,' he said. 'I reckon you've been trained in subversion tactics.'

I giggled a little, as Michael put the kettle on and I reached down the cake tin. It was fun being involved in a police operation, like being in the middle of an episode of 'The Bill'. Although I was expecting it, I felt quite disconsolate when Michael said they would be gone next day.

'Surveillance over,' he explained. 'I'm afraid it's on to the next job.'

It had only been a few days, and I had not even met his fellow officers, but already I felt they were part of my life. I assured Michael I was sworn to secrecy for ever, and when I went down to get the milk next morning they were gone.

I missed Michael, and over the next couple of weeks I thought of him a lot. It was good to reflect that I had been part of helping him in his job, and I consoled myself with this, although it was cold comfort.

It was in the local shop that I got the idea. That Myra with the spindly legs, was putting my shopping in a bag and I said, 'Hang on, I've forgotten something.' I went and got some dried mixed fruit and glace cherries and extra butter.

'Oh, cake making again are we Mrs Jackson?' Myra said in that patronising way she has, pretending to be interested but you know it's false.

'Yes,' I said. 'I'm going to make a cake for my grandson.'

***

When I got to Argyle Street police station I thought I could just leave the cake at the desk, but the chap said to hang on a minute. Then a young woman came to see me and said I'd made a mistake, they didn't have a Michael Robinson there. I realised what had happened and explained that Michael was not one of their regular officers, but was attached to the CID, on secondment from Northern Ireland. When she still insisted there was no-one of that name at the station, on secondment or anything else, I explained patiently that he was on undercover work and suggested that perhaps I could leave the cake with someone from CID.

She looked rather warily at the parcel and then asked me to wait. Eventually I was shown into an office and two policemen, one in uniform and one in plain clothes, started asking me lots of questions. They acted as if Michael didn't exist, and I lost patience.

'Look,' I said. 'He's attached to this station, on secondment from Northern Ireland. You had arranged to use the house next door to mine for surveillance, ask the landlord, Mr. Mason…'

'We already did,' said the one in uniform. 'He knows nothing of these people, the house was empty that week. He had arranged for the painters to come in the following week.'

'Yes, they did…' I said, floundering.

'Mrs Jackson, we believe these men may have taken over the house for bomb making activities. We were expecting something like that in this area, but didn't know where. You may have information which will help us with our enquiries…'

Michael! My lovely Michael! My grandson!

They put a tape in the machine, and I was there for what seemed like hours.

And it wasn't a bit like 'The Bill.'

MOTHER LOVE

It had worked perfectly. I'd left the office at the same time as usual, walked along Cross Street, nipped down the alley and in at the back door of number 14, strangled her, and then had come straight out, and quietly continued my walk to the bus stop. Mind you, I had to fight an almost overwhelming desire to run, but I didn't, and reached the bus stop at almost the same time as usual. It had been so quick, and so easy!

It wasn't until I was on the bus, staring at the drab houses through the window, that I realised the enormity of what I'd done. I glanced around the bus as it shuddered into life. Everything was normal, the same people uttering the same tired monosyllables at the end of the working day. Only I was different. I was a murderer.

For a terrifying moment I thought that everyone on the bus knew. I took a deep breath and forced myself to think rationally. No one knew. In fact, dressed in my navy raincoat and carrying my briefcase, I looked just what I was, a clerk in the Council Tax department at the Town Hall, on his way home from work.

Anyway, she deserved it. I had a momentary thrill of satisfaction. She was dead! The sniggering, patronising Mrs. Oaksey was dead! That would be one in the eye for my mother when she found out!

Mother and I had always been close. Too close, I sometimes thought. My father was killed in a car accident before I was born, so I think my mother thought I was all she had left of her marriage. A distant cousin of mine once told me I was a 'pampered and over protected little monster' as a child, but I think that was an exaggeration, he was probably just jealous. Mother did everything for me, and although we lived in quite a poor area, I always had good clothes and well-polished shoes at school, whereas lots of other kids were really scruffy. My mother used to knit lovely jumpers for me, and always sewed a name label into all my clothes. In fact she still does, although I wish she wouldn't. It makes me feel a bit silly at my age.

I admit that sometimes I have felt slightly annoyed at the degree of control my mother exercises over me. She even chooses my library books, so that I only read what she calls 'suitable' authors. I don't really mind. I know she has my best interests at heart. Sometimes though, I wish I could have a few secrets from her. If I ever have had a secret, she has always found out, and then I have felt guilty. Like the time I took a girl to the cinema two years ago, and someone saw us and told my mother. I thought I would die of embarrassment when mother asked me about it. Of course I didn't see the girl again, as Mother explained she wasn't really a very nice girl, and not suitable for me.

Mother has always understood me completely, which I suppose is why I felt I would like to have something, just one thing, which was a secret from her.

'Well - I've got a secret now alright!' I said to myself as I got off the bus. Something secret from my mother, something she would never know, never find out. And what a secret! I had killed her precious, canting Mrs Oaksey!

As I walked homewards, I still felt a sense of shock as I recalled how Mrs. Oaksey had changed our lives. I had come home from work one day and there she was, large as life, sitting in our living room. The remains of tea and cakes were still on the tea trolley, the one mother and I always use for supper in front of the T.V. They were laughing, and as I stood there in the doorway my mother said:

'Oh it's Derek, I didn't realise it was so late, I must have forgotten the time'.

She hadn't even got my tea ready, and it's always waiting for me when I get home.

Mother told me later that she had met Mrs. Oaksey in a coffee shop in town, and as they got on well together, had asked her round for tea. I was a bit annoyed, but if it had stopped there I certainly wouldn't have had to kill her. However, the next few months were the most painful and frustrating of my life. It seemed Mrs. Oaksey was always around. If she was not at our house, mother was at hers. I often came home to a cold tea on a tray with a note. I told mother I didn't like her spending so much time with her new friend, but she wouldn't listen.

'Don't be silly Derek,' she said. 'Doreen and I are both widows, and our children are grown up, so we can enjoy things together now.'

Yes, - it was 'Doreen' now. 'Doreen' this and 'Doreen' that, I grew sick of the sound of her name. I hated her more each day, and I almost began to hate mother too.

Last Thursday I decided to kill her.

As I arrived home from work and opened the front door, I heard the now familiar chatter coming from the living room. I stopped. They were enjoying themselves so much they hadn't heard me come in, and they were talking about me.

'I've always felt the need to protect Derek,' my mother was saying. 'It's been clear he would never be able to stand on his own feet. That's why I'm so glad he has his job at the Town Hall. It's a dull and boring job, just routine, but he can do it and it keeps him occupied. He'll never get any further of course.'

'No, but it takes all sorts,' said Mrs. Oaksey, 'and there's no harm in him. It's a shame he couldn't have found someone to marry him, it would have taken the burden from you. Mind you, there aren't many girls now who would fancy someone like Derek, they don't go for wimps do they?'

I didn't wait to hear any more. I went out and stood in the porch, shaking with fury. Wimp was I? I'd show them!

After I calmed down I went back into the house, making a noise at the front door so they would think I'd just come in. That evening when they were out old-time dancing I made my plans. I knew where Mrs. Oaksey lived. I walked down Cross Street every evening on my way home from work. During the following week, I killed her a dozen times in my mind, as I planned my strategy.

And today I had done it! I knew Doreen would be at home, as she had to get ready for their usual Thursday night old-time dance. When I knocked at the back door, she obviously thought I had come with a message.

'Oh, - it's you Derek,' she called. 'Come in, it's not locked.'

I didn't give her the chance to cry out. With my hands around her throat I squeezed and squeezed for dear life. For a little old lady she certainly put up quite a struggle. I hadn't realised she would find such strength.

The look of horror on her face flashed vividly before me as I relived those appalling moments. She fought hard, but blindly, hitting out, grabbing at my scarf and lapels, before finally losing consciousness. I made certain she was dead, and then left quickly, making sure I wiped away any fingerprints from the door handles.

Now it was over, and I had to forget it. Everything had gone perfectly.

I stopped at the front porch, and prepared myself to enter the house and act normally. Mother would find out what had happened soon enough, when her precious Doreen didn't turn up at the dance. I opened the door.

'Hello Mother, I'm home.'

'Oh hello dear, have you had a nice day?'

'Yes, same as usual.' I smiled at her.

'I've left you a nice supper on a tray.' She bustled about. 'You remember I'm going ...' she stopped, and her face changed.

'Oh Derek, - where is your scarf? You haven't lost it?'

I looked down. It wasn't there! Mrs. Oaksey's dying struggles flashed before me again. Her terrified eyes, her fingers scrabbling at my scarf ....

'Never mind,' Mother said, 'It's a good job I always sew your name into everything.'

CHRISTO'S LESSON

The girl behind the Boots counter made a show of sympathy. 'No, I'm so sorry,' she said. 'That's the largest pack we have. We aren't allowed to sell them in larger packs any longer.'

As if I didn't know, Mary thought to herself as she handed over the pack of paracetamol for wrapping and fished in her purse for the money. Boots was the third place she had tried and she now had three small packs of paracetamol. Perhaps that was enough, she thought, smiling at the assistant as she put away her change and fought her way through the Christmas shoppers towards the door. *Who the hell made these decisions anyway? Did they really think that if someone had decided to kill themselves, they could be dissuaded by having to buy the tablets a few at a time? It just made it more inconvenient, that was all, like most things these days.*

Out on the pavement she took stock. There was that small pharmacy at the top of Hope Street. She sighed, it was a good walk and she was already feeling tired. She had to call at Tesco anyway and so she could get another small pack there. The trouble was she didn't really know how many it would take. All the tablets she had were standard strength, if only she could have got some really strong ones, of course she would need less. Unfortunately, they were only available on prescription.

As she walked to the car she amused herself by imagining the conversation she would have with her doctor if she asked him for 'plenty of high strength paracetamol.' He was a good doctor; she had to admit that, and would never prescribe anything without a full investigation. Being a nosy parker was probably a good fault in a doctor, she supposed.

She drove onto the Tesco car park and got out of the car wearily. There was a distinct nip in the air and she shivered. The forecasters could be wrong, she thought. It could possibly be a white Christmas.

***

Christo raced his bike to the top of the cul-de-sac and whizzed around the loop in a dazzling display of total control as he stopped dead. The first time he had tried this stunt he had catapulted over the handlebars, but now he had it to a fine art. The only problem was that the bike was becoming too small for him, or rather, as his Dad insisted, Christo was becoming too big for the bike. Well, that would not be a problem for long, at least if Santa did his stuff and came up with a larger bike, one with proper gears, like Jackie Scott's.

He parked his bike carefully behind the shed and went into the kitchen. His mother was there, and as usual she quickly provided him with a mug of milky tea and a piece of bread and jam. This was just to last him until it was time for tea, which they all had together. Christo loved this time each school day, when he had his mother to himself for ten or fifteen minutes until his older sister came in from school.

'Mom,' he said now, biting into the bread and jam, 'Do we know any old people?'

'Of course,' she said, 'There's your Grandpa, he's over seventy.'

'Yes, but he's in Scotland. I mean someone nearer.'

'Why? Why do you want an old person?'

'Well, Mrs Johnson was telling us today about Christmas, what it means and everything. Like you have to be kind to people and help them if you can. Not only at Christmas but especially at Christmas. She said if you know someone who is old and lives on their own, they might need some help. I could perhaps help them to do a job or something.'

His mother smiled at him indulgently. 'Mrs Johnson is absolutely right. Let's think. Well of course there's Mary next door. She's quite old and lives on her own, and a very nice lady. She's been in hospital recently too. She's better now of course, but she might appreciate some help. You could ask her, I'm sure she wouldn't mind.'

'Good thinking, Batman,' Christo said as he slid off the chair. 'I'll go and try her now.'

'Christo!' His mother's voice stopped him at the front door. 'Remember you are offering to help. You don't get paid for that! If Mary offers you fifty pence or a pound or something, you mustn't accept. This isn't like 'Bob-a-Job'.

'O.K.' Christo smiled happily and sped off down the front path.

For Mary it had been another average day. She had lived through it, she had shopped, met acquaintances on the High Street and greeted them with a welcoming smile, life after all was not so bad, her demeanour suggested, and 'yes' she agreed – it really was such a busy time. At home she had put away her few bits of shopping, opened her cards which had arrived by the second post and was grateful. Alone, she had sunk into the chair and picked up the remote control, reaching for the friends she knew on 'Countdown', silently desperate and at a loss. Nevertheless, when the bell rang she was annoyed at the interruption.

Christo stood there, his innocent face wide eyed and beaming.

'Hello, Christo,' Mary said. 'What can I do for you?'

'Do you need help?' asked Christo enthusiastically. 'Can I do a job or something for you?'

'Er – I don't know,' said Mary, slightly taken aback. 'Would you like to come in for a moment? We can have a cup of tea and I'll think about it.' She led the way indoors and Christo followed her, sitting carefully down on the sofa where Mary indicated, and gazing around him with delight and interest.

'I'll put the kettle on,' Mary said, and went into the kitchen. What on earth did the child want? Can I help you? He must be all of eight years old! What a face though! What a truly beautiful child, like one of those angelic choristers you sometimes see, so beautiful you catch your breath in wonder, a face from a Renaissance painting...

She went back into the lounge, and Christo said 'You've got a lovely house haven't you?' He giggled. 'It's very tidy, a lot tidier than ours.'

'Well, there are more people in your house,' Mary said, 'So it's bound to be more untidy.'

'Doesn't look as if you've got any jobs to do,' said Christo. 'I thought I could help you put up your decorations or balloons or something, if you can't reach.'

Mary suppressed a smile. 'I don't put up decorations or balloons any longer,' she said, 'It's not really worth it when you are on your own.'

'Why not?' said Christo.

There didn't seem any answer to that so Mary said, 'There's something I've been meaning to ask you Christo. Your name, it's very unusual isn't it?'

'Yes, but it isn't in South Africa, that's where we are from, did you know that?'

'Yes, your Daddy told me when you moved in.'

'Well, my name is Christ, with an 'o' on the end. Christo. And my Mom's name is Christ with an 'a' on the end. Christa.'

'I see. I'll make the tea.'

Over their mugs of tea Christo talked himself hoarse. He chattered on and on, about his school, and his teacher, about his sister who was at the big school, about his Mum and Dad, and several times Mary had to steer the conversation away from their problems, or Christo would have revealed every family secret. Suddenly he said 'This is a pretty mug.'

'Yes,' Mary said, watching him twist the china mug around in his fingers, gazing at it intently. 'Those flowers on it, they're called fuchsias, have you heard of them?'

'No' said Christo. 'Fuchsias', examining the mug again.

'I have some in my garden, and I think there are some in yours, you'll see them in summer. That one on the mug is named after a famous person. It's called 'Winston Churchill,' – have you heard of him?'

Christo shrugged his shoulders. 'No,' he said, as if bemused.

'Oh. Well.' *I don't think I ever met anyone who hadn't heard of Winston Churchill, she thought.* 'Oh, well, he was a very famous man, he was the Prime Minister during the war, have you heard of the war?'

Christo shrugged again and laughed. 'No,' he said again, totally non-plussed.

He's eight years old you fool! Of course he hasn't heard of Winston or the war!

'Well, never mind, I'll tell you about him another time. You just remember the lovely fuchsia named after him.'

Christo stayed another half hour and they watched the rest of 'Countdown', trying to make up words together. Then Mary escorted him to the door, and thanked him for his offer of help. 'If I have a problem,' she said, 'I'll remember you are there and I will call if I need you.'

'Good,' said Christo happily, 'Just let me know.' He was obviously confident of his abilities. He turned, 'Mary, can we be friends?'

Mary swallowed. 'Of course, Christo,' she said.

'And in the summer will you show me the fuchsias and the other flowers you told me about, the one's in your garden, so I know the names?'

A budding horticulturalist!

'Of course I will, Christo,' she said. 'There's a lot to learn about plants.' On impulse she gave him a kiss. 'Happy Christmas,' she said 'To you and all your family.'

He beamed the beatific smile. 'Happy Christmas Mary!'

When he had gone Mary washed up the mugs and wondered again at his visit.

Can I help you? Can I do a job or something? An eight year old! Still, he's a sweet child, obviously has a caring nature. I hope he manages to keep it as he grows up. Can we be friends? he had asked.

As Mary put away the mugs she caught sight of the bottles of paracetamol on the kitchen table. She sighed, she still didn't know how many she needed. She didn't have to do it tonight anyway, not before Christmas. Perhaps she should write a letter to her cousin in York, her only relative. Wouldn't be so much of a shock then. Suddenly she thought of Christo. Such a dear child. What would he think if his new found friend was found dead one morning? How would his parents explain it to him? Who would show him the fuchsias next summer and tell him the names of the plants? His parents knew nothing of gardening otherwise they would never have pulled out that old clematis soon after they moved in – thought it was dead just because it had died back for winter. Hadn't a clue really.

Mary moved back into the lounge. Nearly time for 'Pointless'. Perhaps she would put up a few decorations after all, just that tiny tree and a few baubles she had stored in the top of the wardrobe. Cheer the place up a bit. What had she been thinking of? Life was not so bad; she had plenty of acquaintances and still had fairly good health. Perhaps she should still write to her cousin in York, they were about the same age and she was on her own too. Perhaps she'd like to come and stay for a week in Spring. It's just this awful weather, she thought, so cold and miserable, but once Christmas is over it won't be long until Spring.

Christo sat watching Mrs Johnson intently. She was talking about Christmas and was asking everyone if they had a nice time, and about the presents they had received, and those they had given.

'And what about our project?' she asked. 'Do you remember before we broke up we were going to see if we could help someone who might need it, perhaps an old person or someone who lived alone? Darren, did you find anyone who needed help?'

'Yes Miss,' said Darren Jones proudly. 'An old lady at the bottom of our street. She gave me a list and I went to the shop for her, and I posted some letters and cards as well.'

'Well done, Darren,' said Mrs Johnson. 'What about you Christo? Did you manage to help anyone?'

'No,' said Christo sadly. 'I tried to. The lady next door, she's good fun. We are friends now and I go to her house sometimes and we talk. But I couldn't help her, she didn't need anything.'

WHITE BEAR LAKE

Purple clouds towered over the Western horizon as I hurried towards White Bear Lake. Already large flakes of soft snow were beginning to blur my vision.

'Damned woman,' I muttered, wishing that my big Gladstone bag was not so heavy. I had left my normal medical bag in the car at Patrick's inlet, the small creek where the last of the fishing boats landed their catch daily. It was the furthest point a wheeled vehicle could make, and after that it was Shank's pony, unless you happened to have a horse in the boot. I changed my fully supplied Gladstone to my other hand and pressed on, sure that at least I was equipped for any emergency.

'Damn the woman,' I thought again. There was probably no emergency at all, and she would send me away with a flea in my ear, as usual.

Margaret Anstey had lived in her old derelict cabin for almost four years, although Jack Ryan, the postman, insisted her name was Margaret Booth, and he should know, coming out here twice a week to deliver. Margaret herself answered to neither name. On her medical record I had written Margaret Anstey-Booth, which gave her an aristocratic connotation she certainly didn't merit. She was not often seen in the village, and when she was, the children called her 'Mad Maggie'. Early this year she went away to Montreal according to the station master, but no-one knew why, and after she returned her pregnancy became increasingly obvious. That's when the real gossip began, and the laughing phrase 'well we know what she's been up to!' went around the village.

I must say I was not surprised when the maternity unit at Greenacre hospital called to say she had not checked in as arranged. It was par for the course, as any pre-natal help I had been able to give had been instigated by me when Margaret's condition became apparent. 'I'll manage,' she had re-iterated vehemently, over and over. 'I don't need any help thank you.' One thing I had been able to establish was that the birth was due any time, certainly within the next week or so, and Margaret being stuck out here in this God forsaken wilderness was not to be contemplated. So much for her promise the last time I saw her. It annoyed me that she seemed to have no idea how much trouble she caused.

By the time I reached the cabin the snow was coming thick and fast, and the sky was threatening a white-out. A huge stack of chopped logs was stored against the cabin front, at least Margaret had got herself prepared for winter. I could not see a light but knocked loudly. When no-one answered I turned the tarnished knob and walked in, adjusting my eyes to the gloom.

Margaret lay in the truckle bed. I could see at once that she was in advanced labour. Her face was flushed and sweaty with exertion. I thought I saw a flicker of relief pass over her face when she saw me, but perhaps I imagined it.

'You pick your time doctor,' she said sarcastically, 'I'm not receiving visitors.'

'Looks as if you'll be receiving one fairly soon, whether you want to or not,' I replied drily. I took her pulse. 'Why didn't you do what we arranged? You only had to get to Patrick's inlet, we'd arranged for Jack Ryan to take you into Greenacre.'

'We arranged nothing. You arranged what you wanted, I never said I'd be there…' She broke off as pain convulsed her.

'Never mind that now,' I said, 'I'd better get started…'

'It may have escaped your notice doctor, but I've started already,' she gasped. 'Those kettles and pans will be nearly boiled dry by now.'

It was true. There was enough hot water on the old stove to launch a battleship, never mind a baby.

'Anything you need is over there,' Margaret said as she subsided into the pillows. 'Under the sheet.'

I had wondered about that sheet last time I visited. There was little enough in the sparsely furnished cabin, and a sheet covered what was on the far wall. I removed it gingerly. A large table was covered with almost everything I could possibly need, including a carry cot, piles of new baby clothes, and even some infant milk 0 - 3 months.

I turned back to Margaret, 'Come on,' I said, 'I'd better examine you properly, you planned this all along didn't you?'

She gasped, and gave me a half-smile. 'I knew you'd come doctor, but I was thinking I'd got it wrong when the baby started. It wasn't supposed to be yet.'

'These things don't always go to order,' I said, 'And it looks like we're going to be snowed in.'

***

Three hours later and all was serene. The dear little boy lay sleeping peacefully in the carry cot, and Margaret and I had at least managed a truce. Now, with her sheets changed and herself washed and comfortable, she gave me her rare smile. She was really quite attractive when she did that.

'You see doctor, I told you it would be all right.'

I came and sat down beside the bed. 'You were lucky,' I said. 'You really should not have taken such a risk'.

'No risk', she said firmly, 'Not when I had the best doctor in the territory with me.'

'Oh yes?' I said, trying not to respond to the flattery.

'That's what I heard said when I came here,' she said. 'Everyone says it and it's true.'

I tried to change the subject. 'Margaret, you have given birth before haven't you? You don't have to tell me if you don't want to, but I know you have.'

She turned her face away, but eventually she said, 'Yes, just over five years ago.' She stopped, and I did not comment, but then she said, 'He died. Six pounds seven ounces and a perfect pregnancy, born in the real hi-tech maternity hospital in Montreal, absolutely everything was fine. And he died....'

As her voice faltered I began to realise perhaps why she was so averse to having her second baby in hospital. 'That is awful,' I said. 'Did they say what it was?'

'Heart defect apparently,' she answered, and then to my increasing concern, 'It was the same hospital where my husband died, three months before the birth.'

'What?' I was horrified, but now Margaret had begun she seemed to want to say it all. 'It was leukemia, Non-Hodgkins Lymphoma to be exact. When we knew it was terminal the hospital was able to save sperm for us. The baby, I called him John after my husband, was conceived by artificial insemination, and at least my husband knew his child was on the way.'

'And you lost them both. Oh my dear...' I could find no words.

'I came here to grieve doctor, I thought I could perhaps find something. Something I was looking for, I don't really know what. I didn't want people, asking me over and over how I was and what I was going to do. I didn't know. I was lost.' Her gaze strayed over to the carry cot. 'I'm not lost now. This place, the serenity, the ocean.... it helped me. There was still sperm left in my name at the sperm bank in Montreal. I went there earlier this year and I was lucky. It worked.' She gave me that rare smile again.

'So this is your husband's baby?' I felt the tears threatening.

'Yes, and this time no problems. I knew it would be all right if I had him here, I just felt it.'

I nodded. Everything in my training denied it, but something deep inside me understood. 'Yes, I think after all you may have been right, but now you have your son—'

'Jamie,' she interrupted, 'I'm going to call him James.'

'Jamie,' I agreed. 'Now you have Jamie he must come first, and although I understand how you feel about hospitals, we must have him checked out properly in Greenacre. I know the maternity staff well, they are very kind and efficient, and it will only take a day or so, and I'll come with you.' I could see she was about to dissent, so I added, 'Anyway, don't think about it now, we all need some sleep, so you rest and I'll make myself a bed up on the couch.'

***

And so it progressed. Over the next two days I managed to contact Jack Ryan and the maternity unit at Greenacre, (thank goodness for mobile phones; I told Margaret I had to go outside the cabin to get a good signal.) I also found a pretext to phone a few ladies in town who I knew were real gossips, I was going to make sure the whole town knew they were wrong about Mad Maggie. Of course I did not divulge anything told me in confidence, but Margaret had not asked me to keep her history secret, and for once in my life I felt that to gossip a little was in my patient's interest. If I'm wrong, well so what? It's not the first mistake I've ever made and it won't be the last.

Although I made my plans quite easily. it was a while before Margaret would agree. In spite of all I said to persuade her, she re-iterated over and over that she and Jamie would be 'just fine' at the cabin once she had regained her strength.

'You have said he's OK doctor, and that's good enough for me.'

'My opinion is that he is completely healthy,' I agreed. 'But I cannot give the kind of reassurance we need. I don't have the right equipment here, or the experience that a proper maternity unit can provide.' I sighed. 'Of course, it's your decision, but it seems to me you have to choose between what you want, and what is right for Jamie.'

With that I shut up, and a few moments later Margaret said 'Of course. We must have him checked at the hospital.'

***

When Jack Ryan arrived on foot, with his brother Will following with his dog team and sled, Margaret and I both broke into laughter. Margaret and the baby went in the sled with my Gladstone bag, and Jack and I followed on foot. He told me the snow plough had got through to Patrick's inlet and so there should be no problem getting to Greenacre. Jack padlocked the cabin before we left, telling Margaret that when she was due to come home he would go in the day before and get the stove going.

'It'll be freezing, and you can't bring Jamie back to a cold cabin,' he said to Margaret, pocketing the key. I had a sudden vision of the future, with Margaret and young Jamie at the cabin for the school holidays in the summer -what a great time they would have.

As we began our journey back to civilisation I turned and looked back at the wild shore, and the snow bound cabin. Those purple clouds were appearing again on the Western horizon, shot with deep pink and a gleam of orange as the sun lowered. Perhaps, I reflected, not such a God forsaken place after all.

THE ANGEL

(1972)

***

It was not far from the cemetery to Grandpa Jack's cottage, and so after the funeral, they walked back. Assorted villagers and friends watched them go, little Mary, only six, holding tight to Nana Ellen's hand, serious at first, but unable to stop the inevitable skip and hop as she realised she had escaped the sad business of the day. Her brother Jimmy, who was just eleven, was more aware, and although he strode out bravely, many people noticed the grubby tear tracks on his face. He held tightly onto Grandpa Jack's hand as they made their way home. As they reached the cemetery gates a large car pulled alongside and stopped.

'Jack!' The electric window had opened. 'Can we give you a lift?'

Grandpa Jack crossed to the car. 'That's kind Mr Driscoll.' He nodded to the driver, the elderly owner of the Driscoll estate, who had been his employer for over forty years. Now Jack was retired he did not address him as 'sir', but still, he would have felt uneasy using his first name. He nodded again to the well preserved lady in the passenger seat, dressed impeccably as always in her 'designer mourning' clothes, topped by the inevitable large hat in black and grey.

'Hello Mrs Driscoll,' Jack said. 'Good of you to come.' He realised he had said that before, as they came out of church, but what else did you say? 'Er, no...we won't have a lift if you don't mind, the children need a bit of fresh air and it will be good to walk.'

'Of course, we'll let you get on.' Mr Driscoll smiled, then 'Jack, if there's anything, anything at all...'

'I know sir, thank you.'

The 'sir' had slipped out. Habit of course.

'We were both very fond of your son,' Mrs Driscoll leaned over, but before she could say anything else her husband added, 'He was the best gamekeeper I ever had, apart from his Dad of course.' His eyes were kind as he closed the window, and as the car pulled away Jack told himself that old man Driscoll was showing genuine concern. It was easy to feel oneself patronised, but he must guard against that when it was not intended.

'Come on lad,' he said to Jimmy, taking his hand again. 'Nana will get us some tea, I expect there will be cake.'

There was not going to be a formal 'after funeral' gathering, Jack had put his foot down. 'It's only an opportunity for some to gawp,' he had said when Ellen had suggested it. 'You know there is no money for it and even if we catered it ourselves, it's too much for you.'

It was true. The devastation left by the car crash which had killed his son and his lovely wife had been unbearable, for himself and for Ellen, and most of all for the two children now in their charge. All of them were crushed and exhausted, but somehow they all made an effort to be strong, for themselves and each other.

As he opened the front door of the cottage, Jack heard the familiar chime of the old long case clock in the hall. Four o'clock. Time to move on.

***

Two days later Jack and Ellen were 'having words.' The visit from Social Services hadn't helped. Did that woman really think they believed all that sweet talking nonsense about 'only being there to help,' when it was obvious to anyone she was 'on the snoop?'

'She thinks we can't take care of the children,' Jack complained again.

'She's only doing her job,' Ellen countered. 'Jimmy, Mary, you can go out to play for a bit, put your coats on.' She helped Mary with the toggles on her duffel coat. 'You can bring me a piece of heather if you like,' she said. 'There's lots up on the hill, but don't go too far.'

When they had gone she turned to Jack. 'You must remember not to talk like that in front of them,' she said. 'They're feeling insecure enough as it is without you making it worse.'

'That woman thought we were too old for the job,' Jack exploded. 'It was obvious!'

'And you telling her we both aimed to live for another ten years helped, did it?' Ellen asked sweetly. 'Sarcasm never helps, love.'

***

Jimmy and Mary had not gone up onto the hill, but round the back of the cottage to their own special bolt-hole. Many years ago it had been a pig sty, but cleaned out it was a good place for drinking pop and doing some of Jimmy's experiments from his chemistry set. Lately, they had come here just to talk.

'I don't care,' Mary was saying crossly, 'I don't want Mummy and Daddy there under the ground. They shouldn't be there.'

Jimmy sighed. Would she never understand?

'Of course they should,' he said kindly. 'It's what happens when you're dead.'

'Well...they shouldn't be dead...' Mary bleated. She looked as if she was going to cry again.

'But it's happened,' Jimmy tried to reassure her. 'We can't make it not happen.'

Mary nodded sadly. 'I know, I wouldn't mind if there was an angel.'

'What angel?'

'Like those in the cemetery. You know...big angels...they have wings and are saying their prayers. When I was frightened of the dark, Mummy told me it was alright because my angel was looking after me in the night, so we should have an angel looking after them.'

Jimmy nodded. 'Well, perhaps there is an angel looking after them, you can't always see angels.'

'You can in the churchyard, there are some lovely big ones. We'll ask Grandpa if we can have one for Mummy and Daddy to look after them.'

'We can't, because I heard Nana Ellen talking about it, they cost a lot of money and we haven't got any because of no surrance.'

Mary stared doubtfully. 'What's surrance?'

'It's something that when you're dead, other people get money. But we don't. Grandma said perhaps a little stone later on. I expect angels cost thousands of pounds.'

'Well I want an angel!' Mary yelled, threatening tears again. 'They ought to have an angel...'

'I'll think of something,' Jimmy said. 'Don't cry, we'll get the money somehow, leave it to me.'

'You promise?' Mary smiled tearfully.

'I promise,' Jimmy said, and Mary smiled again and ran off to get Nana Ellen some heather.

***

After Mary had gone to bed that night Jimmy accosted his Grandpa, who was reading the paper.

'Grandpa, Mary wants us to have an angel for Mom and Dad's grave,' he said. 'You know, with a nice face and big wings and saying their prayers.'

'Ah, it's called a memorial Jimmy, but we can't do that, perhaps a stone later, with your Mom and Dad's names on it.'

'But Mary wants an angel, so they'll be looked after, couldn't we sell something?'

'Nothing to sell lad, well, at least...' Grandpa sighed and folded his paper. 'Come with me Jimmy, have I ever showed you this?'

Jimmy followed him into the hall.

'You know our family have been gamekeepers on the estate for over 150 years? Well this clock was given to my great grandfather by the man who owned the estate then. Nothing to do with the Driscoll's, they bought the estate after the war. But this clock is very old... see here, you can see the makers name...it says William Troutbeck of Leeds, and the year 1725. It's made of walnut and not many folks have a clock like this I can tell you. It's our family heirloom, and very precious, and one day it will be yours.'

'Is Daddy's gun worth a lot of money?'

'Your Dad's shotgun? Well, a fair bit I suppose, you know it is yours now, but I've locked it away in my gun cupboard. When you are old enough I'll teach you to shoot.'

'I already can. Well, a bit. Dad showed me how to load it and let me have a couple of tries, he said I can learn properly when I leave school.'

'That's right,' said Jack. 'But in case you're wondering, even if we sold your Dad's shotgun it wouldn't be enough for a memorial, not one with a big angel on it anyway.'

By the time he went to sleep Jimmy had worked it out, his Dad used to make money shooting pheasants, and he could do the same. He wondered how many he would have to shoot to buy an angel, and hoped the man in Trowbridge who had bought them from his Dad would buy them from him.

The next afternoon Jimmy waited until Grandpa Jack and Nana Ellen were both working on the vegetable patch while Mary had her nap. Then he crept into the kitchen and there they were, Grandpa Jack's keys on the dresser, where he always left them. He took the keys and went to the gun cupboard and unlocked the outer and then the inner doors, and took out his father's shotgun. He opened the small drawer at the bottom and found the ammunition, he knew the right ones by the box. He stuffed them in his pocket quickly and re-locked the gun cupboard. Then he returned the keys to the dresser and made his way up the hill, from where he knew he could see the undulating edges of the pheasants nesting sites. There were hundreds of them up there, and he was sure he could get plenty.

***

Mrs Driscoll strode out purposefully. She was walking faster than usual on her afternoon stroll, as she had read an article in The Times supplement that showed that the faster you walked, the more calories you burned. She would never have resorted to actual running, but still, one had to make an effort. Today she was wearing her 'aristocracy on a country weekend' outfit, tweed skirt and jacket, cashmere jumper and tan walking shoes, and of course the small trilby style hat with long feathers. She heard some shots nearby, and realised uneasily that it might be poachers, no one should be out with a shotgun at this time. The next moment the top of her head seemed to explode, and as she sank dizzily to the ground she saw through a haze, fragments of feathers drifting lazily around her.

***

Grandpa Jack, with Jimmy and Mary in tow, were shown into the library, where Mr and Mrs Driscoll were waiting. Both men had agreed on the telephone how to approach the matter, and a glance passed between them.

'Good afternoon,' said Grandpa Jack, his tone very serious. 'My grandson Jimmy has something to say to you.' He pushed Jimmy forward.

'I'm very sorry,' said Jimmy sullenly. He didn't sound sorry, and Grandpa Jack nudged him. 'I didn't mean to shoot anybody, honestly.' He looked at Mrs Driscoll. 'I'm sorry about your hat, I didn't see you, I could only see your hat because you were behind the hill, I thought it was a pheasant.'

'You shouldn't have been shooting pheasants anyway,' said Driscoll. 'They're my pheasants, and anyway you aren't old enough.'

'Sorry.' Jimmy mumbled again.

Mrs Driscoll tried to help. 'Mary?' she said, 'Do you have something to say as well?'

Mary glanced at her. 'You shouldn't have dead things on your head,' she said. 'They should be in the graveyard.'

'Well perhaps.'

Jack said 'Tell Mr and Mrs Driscoll you will never do such a thing again.'

'We won't do it again,' they chorused.

'Good,' said Mrs Driscoll. 'Now come into the kitchen with me, you can have some orange juice and I'll see if there's some cake.'

***

That evening, when Nana Ellen had finally got Mary into her nightie, she brought her into the kitchen where Grandpa Jack and Jimmy were still sitting after the evening meal.

'Before you go to bed, we have something to do,' said Grandpa Jack. 'I have a catalogue here, it has some lovely memorials in it, and we have to choose one for your Mom and Dad's grave.'

'Do they have angels on?' Mary asked.

'There are some lovely angels,' said Grandpa Jack. 'We'll look through it together and choose the one you like best.'

'I thought we couldn't have one,' said Jimmy, amazed.

'Well, perhaps an angel would be a very special family heirloom after all,' said Jack.

***

As he lay in bed that night, Jack listened intently as the long case clock in the hall struck twelve. After the auctioneer came tomorrow, he would not hear it again; but Mary's laughter was a lovely sound.

If you have enjoyed these stories, please consider putting a review on Amazon.

You may also enjoy Helen Spring's novels:

'*The Chainmakers*.' A family adventure story set in the Black Country of the UK, France and New York.

'*Strands of Gold*.' An adventure story set in colonial Singapore and Australia at the time of the gold rush.

'*Memories of the Curlew*.' A fictionalized account of the life of Gwenllian, known as the Welsh Warrior Princess.

'*Blood Relatives*.' The sequel to 'The Chainmakers' set in wartime Rome and New York.

www.ingramcontent.com/pod-product-compliance
Lightning Source LLC
LaVergne TN
LVHW051954060526
838201LV00059B/3647